Here Without You

By Jennifer L. Allen

Published: Jennifer L. Allen 2017
jenniferlallenauthor@gmail.com
Editor: Aimee Lukas
Cover Design: Concierge Literary Designs & Photography
Cover Photo: The Image Apothecary

Dedication

*To the men and women of the
United States Armed Forces.
Thank you for your service.*

~ **Prologue** ~

Anna

"The lavender gown looks gorgeous on you. It brings out the grey in your eyes. So pretty," I told my sister as she held up her two favorite dresses. The silver dress washed out her pale skin and light blonde hair, but the lavender had just the right contrast, and it made her hazel eyes pop.

I made a mental note to remember that when I went shopping for my prom dress the next week. My older sister was my fashion plate. If it wasn't for me having our dad's nose and her having our mom's, we could have been mistaken as twins; in fact, we sometimes were. Throughout the years, I'd observed and copied her fashion choices, using variations of her styles—and her hand-me-downs—on myself. She never minded, we were as close as two sisters could be. Irish twins, born eleven months apart in the same year. We were even in the same grade. Weird, yes. But it was our normal, and I wouldn't have it any other way.

She smiled sweetly at me. "Thanks, Anna. Derek will be thrilled I can finally give him a color for his tie and vest." Derek was her boyfriend of six months. He was the star quarterback and she was the cheer captain. They were the cliché golden couple of Lakeside High School.

"Don't forget the corsage," I sang as I

removed the dresses she didn't like from the dressing room. "I'm going to put these up, and then I'll meet you in shoes."

"I think I'm just going to wear that silver pair with the kitten heel that I wore to homecoming. Think those will go?" she asked, holding up the floor-length, beaded lavender gown and looking at herself in the mirror. She's going to look amazing all done up in that dress.

I nodded. "Absolutely, I was going to suggest silver."

"Perfect," she said with a decisive nod. "I'm going to head over to cosmetics, I'm about to run out of lipstick. How about we meet over at the coffee shop in ten? I'm dying for a mocha."

"Sounds good," I walked off with the six gowns carefully balanced over my arm.

"Thanks for doing this with me today," she called to me.

"Anytime," I answered, waving at her over my shoulder.

"You're my favorite sister!" she continued.

I laughed and turned to face her, walking backwards. "I'm your only sister! I love you, too, Ronnie."

She smiled at me again and turned in the opposite direction, a bounce in her step as she hustled off to the cosmetic counter, the gown flowing in her wake. I shook my head, turned back around, and proceeded to return the dresses to where we'd found them.

As I placed the final dress on its rack, my phone chimed a new text message.

Ryan.

Beaming, I read my boyfriend's words.

Ryan: I miss you. Still at the mall?
Me: Just finished dress shopping. Going for coffee.
Ryan: Would you be pissed if I crashed your girls day?
Me: Never!
Ryan: I'm finishing up at the shoe store. See you in a few.

I grinned the entire way to the food court.

***

Pulling out a chair out from one of the tables in front of Digital Grinds, I set mine and Ronnie's mochas on the table. Ryan didn't like coffee, so I knew he'd show up with his beverage of choice: some kind of smoothie or an ice cold lemonade. He was a sucker for sweet, fruity drinks. I relaxed back in my seat, eager to spend a few minutes checking out the shoppers while I waited for my sister and Ryan.

The coffee shop slash cyber café was bustling with people. Its location—caddy corner to the food court in Lakeside Mall—allowed me the perfect vantage point for people watching. I loved people watching; they absolutely fascinated me. It was one of the reasons my artistic specialty had always been portraits, sometimes straightforward and sometimes abstract. I loved portraying people on canvas in my own creative style, the same way I assumed photographers enjoyed capturing them on film.

The mall was a hotbed of activity, ripe for my perusal. Packs of girls roamed the wide corridors carrying long plastic garment bags presumably holding formal gowns similar to the one my sister had just purchased. There were trendy women in their tunics, leggings, and ballet flats pushing strollers holding children of various ages and temperaments. The handles of the strollers were laden with paper and plastic shopping bags.

Sometimes I wished I was a photographer, so I could get the instant gratification of capturing their expressions right on the spot. I'd often have to hold images in my memory and hope that later on, I'd be able to convey what I'd seen.

I pulled my cell phone out of my black Coach wristlet and checked the time on the screen. It had been twenty minutes since I left Ronnie. She was late...probably still at the cosmetic counter. I knew she wouldn't leave there with just a lipstick. My sister wasn't vain, she just loved her makeup. And I didn't mind it one bit because she took all the work out of it for me. What looked good on her, looked good on me, by default. Ryan would get here eventually, he was probably purchasing his shoes and picking up his smoothie.

As I tore my eyes from a couple chasing their little boy around the small indoor play area, I finally caught sight of Ronnie walking across the food court from the direction of the department store and waved just as a loud bang shattered the steady, happy din of the mall.

It sounded like someone had set off a firecracker.

In the mall.

Right behind me.

Then the screaming began.

Eyes wide, I stood from my chair and dared to look through the plate glass window of the coffee shop. Through the cheerful Valentine's display in the shop window, I saw the barista I'd just purchased our lattes from with her back pressed against the cappuccino machine behind the counter, hands in the air. Tears were streaming down her face. *What the hell was going on?* Across from her was a guy in a black sweatshirt and jeans. His back was towards me, so I couldn't see his face, but he was gesturing wildly at the girl and...was that a gun in his hand?

The pieces fell together. Blood spatter on the baristas white shirt, the bang, the gun.

He'd shot someone.

As I backed away from the window, another two shots rang out, causing me to jump. One shattered the glass right in front of me. I jumped back another step, frozen in place. I couldn't see the barista anymore. But the guy with the gun...he was still there...and he was looking right at me.

"Anna!"

I followed the sound of my sister's horrified scream and spun on my heels to run towards her. To get the hell away from the disaster that was unfolding just feet away from me.

More shots rang out, and I swore I felt one whiz right by my head before I was tackled to the ground under a large, hard body.

I screamed and kicked and punched my attacker; my survival instinct pressed into full gear.

"Calm down," a deep, gravelly voice said. *Ryan.* "Stay down, baby. I got you."

"R-ronnie," I stammered through chattering teeth, desperately trying to raise my head and look over to where my sister had just been standing.

Ryan put his hand over my head and tucked me safely into his chest and under his body. "She'll be okay, Anna...just wait."

More shots rang out, and my body jolted with every one of them. I was shaking from head to toe, unsure if I was going to throw up or wet my pants. Tears blurred my vision, and I was struggling to breathe. Whether from Ryan's weight on top of me or the panic, I wasn't sure. Probably the panic.

Seconds...minutes...hours went by, for all I knew, while I stayed huddled under the safety of Ryan, breathing in the comfortable, familiar scent that I knew was his Old Spice deodorant.

But...Ronnie.

She was out there.

"P-please...I n-need my s-sister."

He held me tighter, knowing I was going to bolt the moment I felt his grip weaken. He kept shushing me and whispering words to soothe me as absolute hell was taking place nearby.

Then there was silence.

An eerie kind of silence.

There was no movement. No shuffle of bodies or clatter of silverware.

Then a sob.

More sobs.

And suddenly, wails of terror and pain echoed throughout the food court.

I felt Ryan rise and his hold on me lessen. I panicked. I didn't want to be left alone.

What if the guy was still out there?

"N-no. S-stay with m-me. D-don't let me g-go. P-please."

"It's okay," he whispered. "Stay right here. Just for a minute, okay? Let me check things out. I'm not leaving you. I'm just going to look up for a minute."

I nodded, still somewhat pressed against his chest.

He released me and got to his knees. I picked up my head slowly and carefully, noticing for the first time where we'd landed after he knocked me down—tucked behind a few of the trash bins where diners could deposit their trays after their meals.

I peered up at my boyfriend—my rescuer— and I'd never seen the expression on his face before. He looked horrified—sick even—as his eyes darted around the vast space.

Then I remembered Ronnie.

I tore my eyes away from Ryan and searched for my sister. She must have taken cover when she'd realized what was happening. People were huddled under tables, hiding behind trash bins and planters, only a few daring to peek out to see if the danger was still present. I hoped Veronica had retreated, finding her way into one of the nearby stores or hidden somewhere safe.

Then I spotted the edge of a hot pink purse...one that looked remarkably like the Kate Spade purse Ronnie had gripped in her hand just a few moments ago.

My pulse throbbed in my skull.

Maybe she'd dropped it.

"Veronica," I called out quietly. "Ronnie?"

I saw a brown suede ankle boot peeking out from behind a couple of overturned chairs near the purse.

No.

No, no, no.

"Ronnie?" I called out, desperation clouding my voice. I rose to my feet. I had to get to her.

I jumped as a hand landed on my shoulder. It was Ryan. "Anna, you shouldn't..."

"Ronnie is over there!" I yelled, swatting his hand away and taking off. I weaved through the tables, chairs, and mess of food that speckled the floor.

I dropped to my knees beside my beautiful sister's unmoving body, ignoring the sharp pain radiating from my knees at the hard landing.

Her eyes were closed. The front of her jeans and pink short-sleeve blouse appeared clean and untouched. But dark red blood pooled beneath her, seeping into the silver garment bag that held her brand new prom dress.

"Ronnie," I whispered, placing my ice cold hand on her warm cheek. "Ronnie...please wake up."

The small paper bag containing her lipstick lay abandoned near her right hand, and her left hand still gripped the handles of her Kate Spade purse.

I took her right hand in mine and squeezed.

"Ronnie," I cried softly, over and over again. I felt Ryan's arms wrap around my shoulders as I sat there, begging my sister,

"Please wake up."
   "Please wake up."
   "Please wake up."

~ 1 ~

Anna

Five Years Later

I rubbed my hands against my arms, trying to get warm as I walked the cold streets of Seattle. I wished I'd remembered to bring my gloves; it was bad enough I only had a fleece to keep me warm since I'd torn my only winter coat. A new coat wasn't an expense I could afford, not if I wanted to eat and pay rent.

I startled, hearing a scuffle down the dark alleyway I was passing. I didn't turn my head and look, just kept on moving, hastening my pace. I was almost to the bus stop. I could see it through the fine mist my breath was making in front of my face.

At first, I'd been attracted to Seattle's colder weather. It numbed me when all I wanted was to not feel anything. Now, I hated it. I hated everything about it.

I hated the cold.

I hated barely being able to make ends meet.

I hated that I had to walk around with a small switchblade in my pocket just in case some creep tried to attack me.

I hated my apartment and the empty refrigerator inside it.

I hated my job.

I hated the bus.

I hated being so completely and utterly alone.

10

I wanted...I wanted to go home.

I tried not to think about home often. About my parents and my sister...and Ryan, who I knew wasn't even there anymore. Thinking about home made me think about the shooting and everything that happened after. Everything I'd lost.

But I was at the end of my rope. I'd been on my own, wandering around with no direction for far too long. I left Lakeside hoping to find myself, to find *something*. Instead, I'd found nothing but one struggle after another.

My own shame kept me from returning. I knew my parents would welcome me home, but I was too afraid to make the first move, even if it was as simple as picking up the phone and calling them. I let them down so much, I didn't deserve their love.

I sighed as I continued to shuffle down the sidewalk, another cloud of breath appearing before me. One of the many downfalls of working the late shifts at the diner was having to make the trek on the dark streets to the bus stop. I tried to time it just right, so I'd arrive about the same time as the bus and not have to wait alone in the dark bus shelter.

I passed a few bars and night clubs as I walked, excusing myself through a pack of smokers near a designated smoking area.

"Hey," one of them called out as I passed.

I ignored the male voice. The drunks were always so mouthy. Not sure what kind of thrill this guy was looking for, and I wasn't interested either. Surely he wasn't attracted to me in my pale blue polyester diner dress, white tights, and non-skid shoes. I didn't make a pretty picture, and I liked it that way. I generally repelled anyone I came into contact with, with my ghost-like complexion and poor, thrift store fashion choices.

"Anna," the guy called out again, and I froze in place.

This time the voice sounded familiar, but...

No, it couldn't be.

He sounded different. Huskier, maybe? Stronger? Like what the man would sound like, not the boy I remembered.

I contemplated turning around. I knew I should, so I could catch one last glimpse of him...if it was him...but I didn't. I started walking again, quicker than before.

It was a hallucination. I was homesick and imagining things. Great. Was that a symptom of malnutrition?

Hurried footsteps came up behind me, and I reached into my pocket for my knife, about to break into a jog. The bus stop loomed in the distance, so close and yet so far away, when a firm hand landed on my arm and stopped me in my tracks.

I'd felt him just before he touched me...the connection was *still* there...after all that time.

"Anna?" he asked, his voice cracking and sounding more like the boy whose heart I'd broken so many years ago.

"Ryan," I whispered.

He spun me around and looked into my eyes, a frown marring his face as he took me in. I knew what he was seeing: pale skin, bony cheeks, and sunken, lifeless hazel eyes. I was skinny, skinnier than I'd been when I'd last seen him, and I didn't have much extra

12

weight on me back then. I probably looked so frail and breakable to someone like him.

He looked amazing. My eyes darted across his face as I took in the light stubble on his jawline, his high and tight haircut, and serious eyes accented by dramatic eyebrows. The boy turned into a man, and a handsome one at that. He was big...muscular, too. He filled out the chest of his grey long-sleeved t-shirt, and the sleeves of his unzipped coat hugged his biceps. His jeans were loose in some spots, but tight around his thighs and calves.

His study of me was unnerving, it was like he was memorizing every last bit of me. I cowered under his scrutiny, which only made his frown deepen. Huddling down into my too thin fleece, I looked anywhere but at him, hating that he was seeing me like that. What did he think of me?

Ryan didn't say another word, just tugged on the arm that was still in his grasp and pulled me into his chest. He wrapped one arm around my shoulders and the other around my waist and held me tight. He didn't let go for several long minutes. So long that I heard the bus come and go a few paces away. I didn't want to leave his embrace either.

It felt like...home. I missed home.

"Jesus, Anna," he said finally, rubbing my back and running a hand through my hair. "I never thought I'd see you again."

I wanted to return the sentiment, but I couldn't speak. I was still so entranced by this moment.

He pulled away from me, and I was cold once again. "Don't cry," he said, using his thumbs to wipe under my eyes. I hadn't realized I was crying. "What are you doing here? Do you live nearby?"

I shook my head, still not finding my voice.

He looked at my clothes. "Are you just leaving work? Can I walk you to your car?"

"I don't have a car," I said, breaking my silence. His brows furrowed in question, and I responded, "I take the bus."

"That bus?" he asked, pointing his thumb over his shoulder at the bus driving farther down the street.

I nodded.

"I'm sorry," he said, remorse filling his voice.

Shrugging, I told him it was okay. And, oddly, it was okay. Had I not been with Ryan, had I been alone—or worse, with someone else—I would have been in a full on panic. With him I felt safe. I always had.

He grabbed the back of his neck with his hand and looked strained. "I'd offer you a ride, but I don't have a car here. I'm only in town for a few days. A buddy of mine is getting married," he explained, nodding back to the group of guys standing in front of the bar.

"I can call a cab," I said, even though the fare would diminish the tips I made tonight. I really couldn't afford it, but I couldn't exactly walk home, not in this weather at least.

"Can we go somewhere and talk first? Maybe grab some coffee?" he asked. Then he chuckled. "I feel like if I let you out of my sight, I'll never see you again. Your parents have been worried sick about you. I...I've been worried, too."

Coffee was the last thing I wanted after serving it throughout my shift at the diner. Why people got coffee in the evening was beyond me anyway. I didn't think it was wise to have that much caffeine at night.

"I don't really want coffee," I admitted quietly.

"Yeah...me either. I just don't want to let you go yet."

I'd spent five years building a wall around my heart, and in one short moment, he cracked it. Just a small, tiny fissure, but it was there.

"Your friends—"

"They can wait," he cut me off, his firm tone leaving no room for negotiation.

I glanced over his shoulder at his friends. They were all built similarly to him, probably guys he knew from the Navy. They were looking our way, not trying to hide their interest. Subtly was not their strong suit.

"We can go to your place," he offered, but quickly changed directions when my eyes widened, and I began to shake my head. "Or my hotel...it's right around the corner. There's a seating area off the lobby. We can just talk."

"Yeah...okay," I agreed, and he smiled a bright Ryan smile. I missed those smiles.

"Let me just tell the guys. I'll be right back. Don't go anywhere," he held his hands out in front of him, handling me like an animal control agent would manage a wounded dog.

He jogged over to his friends, speaking to them and gesturing to me. They looked my way and nodded, patting him on the back before walking into the bar. Then he jogged back up the sidewalk to me, reaching out his hand.

"You ready?"

Was I ready? I wasn't sure, because I knew...*I just knew*...everything was about to change.

~ 2 ~

Ryan

Holding Anna's hand tightly in mine, I led her to my hotel. I kept looking behind me, making sure it really was her, and she was really here.

My Anna.

No, not my Anna, I corrected myself. Not anymore.

Mikey wasn't exactly thrilled when I told him I was leaving his bachelor party for a woman, but when I'd explained who the woman was, his eyes widened in surprise. He knew all about Anna—all the guys did—and they understood my need to be with her right now.

She looked so different...so unwell. Five years ago, she looked like she had been through hell, but today...I wasn't sure I wanted to know what she'd been doing since she was gone. I didn't think I could handle it. The idea of her struggling...*suffering*...it was all too much.

I pulled her through the sliding doors and into the seating area off to the side of the lobby, and the warmth of the space began to thaw me out. Seattle in December was no joke. Anna must have been freezing in that little fleece jacket she wore. I led her to a small round table with two low chairs.

When she sat down, her shoulders slumped forward and she kept her hands in her lap. She was so withdrawn and skittish. I was afraid that one wrong word or move on my part would send her running; now that I'd found her, I wasn't letting her get away. I was determined to get her back home to her parents. They'd been absolutely sick with worry since she disappeared. Ronnie said she'd needed to get away, but that was bullshit. She hadn't been present enough back then to need to get away.

Anna wanted to hide, and I'd be damned if I was going to let her hide for another minute. It was the end of the road for all that.

"Do you want something to eat or drink?" I asked. The lobby had a small market with soft drinks and snacks.

She shook her head in response, still avoiding eye contact. I'd fix that.

"Can you look at me?"

She stiffened slightly, then lifted her head and looked at me. Hazel eyes that used to sparkle shades of gold and green gazed back at me dully. She looked...hollow.

"Are you okay?" I had to know

She nodded, still not speaking.

"Can you talk to me?"

"What do you want me to say?" she asked, her voice low and quiet. She sounded like her, only different. Worn out--defeated.

"Anything. Tell me anything. Where have you been?"

She looked down to her lap again. She was twisting her hands roughly in her lap, and I was afraid she'd break a finger. Why was she so nervous?

"A few places," she finally answered. "I've been in Seattle almost three years now."

"Three years, wow. You must like it here," I offered, just trying to get her to keep talking.

"It's okay," she shrugged. She was trying to act indifferent, but I knew better. At least I used to.

"How are you really, Anna? Are you okay?"

When her bottom lip quivered, I was ready to jump out of my chair and hold her. I'd always hated seeing Anna upset, but at that moment, she was like a frightened cat. I was terrified she'd spook, then run off to disappear again.

"Yes," she whispered.

Liar.

"Anna...we've known each other a long time. You know I can tell when you're lying to me."

She froze.

"I'm not here to harm you, you know that, right? I just want to help you."

She nodded. It was slight, but it was there, and I took that as a small win.

"Are you safe?" I asked, not sure I was ready for the answer.

"Yes," she answered.

I exhaled with relief. "That's good. That's really good." I took in what she was wearing, an old-fashioned diner dresses. "You work at a diner?" I prodded.

"Yes."

Still with the one word responses. She wasn't making this easy.

"Your parents really miss you. Ronnie, too."

"You still talk to them?" she asked, her voice soft.

"Once a month I call to check in."

She met my eyes, hers questioning. "Every month?"

I nodded. "Just about."

"Why?" she asked. I didn't know why she was so surprised. I'd always been close with her parents.

"To see if they've heard from you. You should call them. The emails you send aren't enough."

She looked down again. "I wouldn't even know what to say," she said eventually.

"Hi. I love you. Fuck off. I'm pretty sure they'd be so excited to hear your voice, they wouldn't even care what the words were."

"They reply to my emails...but I don't read them."

"Why not?" I asked, hoping I wasn't pushing her too hard.

"Because I don't want to feel." She said the words so quietly; I almost wasn't sure if she'd said them at all.

"Don't want to feel what?"

"Anything."

Watching a tear fall from her eye down to her lap, I couldn't resist anymore. I stood from my chair and moved the short distance around the table to her. Kneeling down, I pulled her into my arms. Once she was in the safety of my embrace, she broke down. Big sobs wracked through her body and she trembled. I whispered assurances in her ear and rubbed her back, but it didn't seem like she'd ever stop.

She was breaking my heart all over again.

"I'm so sorry," she choked out.

"Don't be. You have no reason to be sorry."

"I hate my life, Ryan. I thought I knew

what I wanted, but I have no clue. I'm lost, so incredibly lost. I don't know what to do. I'm all alone."

"You're not alone, A," I took a risk, using her nickname, but she didn't pull away. "I'm here. I want to help you, if you'll let me."

"I..." she trailed off.

"What?" I asked, pulling back and placing my fingers under her chin to lift her face. The desolate look in her eyes almost did me in.

"I want to go home," she said, as more tears spilled from her eyes.

Gutted our moment was ending so soon, I nodded and began to rise. "I can get you a cab."

She shook her head. "No, not to my apartment. I want to go *home*."

Realization dawned on me when she stressed the word "home." She wanted to return to Lakeside, to her family. Unable to hold back, I grinned and kissed her forehead. "Then let's get you home."

"But I..." she hesitated.

"What is it?"

"I don't have the money," she said, studying the faux wood tabletop.

"I'll take care of it."

"I can't let you do that."

"You're not *letting* me do anything. I'm offering. I want to." My tone left no room for argument, fortunately she seemed to understand that. If money was the only thing stopping her from returning home, I'd simply remove that obstacle. There once was a time when I would have done anything for this girl, and my actions that night, along with the feeling in my gut, made me question whether

21

that had changed at all.

"What if they don't want me back?" Her voice was barely louder than a whisper.

Shaking my head at her, I chuckled. Either she was trying to come up with excuses not to face the past, or she really had no clue. "Have you been listening to me at all? Your family misses you. They've been crazy with worry. Trust me, Anna. All they want is for you to come home."

She blinked and a few more tears dropped down her cheeks, then she nodded.

I stood and reached a hand out to her. "Let's go home."

~ **3** ~

Anna

The flight attendant's voice came over the speaker, asking passengers to lift their tray tables and stow their belongings in preparation for landing. I didn't have to follow her directions as I did nothing the entire flight but wring my hands, a nervous habit I'd picked up the moment I sat in the cab that took me away from Lakeside.

Ryan put away his laptop and snapped his tray back in place. He glanced over at me, then silently took my hand.

"It'll be okay. They'll be thrilled," he said after a moment.

Nodding absently, I thought about my family. My parents didn't know I was coming. I'd asked Ryan not to call them. I didn't tell him it was because I didn't want them to have any false hope. I made the decision to go home, and I was on the plane, but that was only half the battle. I still had to make it to their house from the airport.

"Seriously, Anna. Whatever you're afraid of...don't be. Your family loves you."

Ryan had been so good to me since he found me on the sidewalk a couple nights ago. He cut his weekend with his friends short to take the cross country flight with me. Leaving me at my apartment the night he'd found me, he promised he'd be back after the wedding the next day, and that we'd catch the

23

first flight out. If he hadn't been a groomsman in the wedding, he would have taken me home that moment.

I was thankful he had to attend the wedding because, to be honest, I'd needed the time to get my head straight. Everything happened so quickly—*changed* so quickly—since I'd bumped into him on the street. I'd felt like I was trapped in a washing machine stuck on the spin cycle. I needed time to process the fact that I was going home, and I needed to tie up my few loose ends.

While Ryan was at the wedding, I spent the day packing my few meager belongings. The furniture, appliances, and kitchenware belonged to the apartment, so I didn't have much. I packed some of my clothes into a backpack and set the rest of the things I'd accumulated over the years—the rest of my clothes and some linens—into a trash bag, which I dropped in a donation bin near my apartment. I also gave notice to my landlord and boss. Neither had cared much—I had a month-to-month lease on the small studio apartment, and my boss was used to people coming and going.

Ryan had shown up at midnight, and we took a cab to the airport. He purchased tickets for the next flight out—one that left first thing in the morning—and after a quick changeover in Atlanta, we were getting ready to land in Lakeside. It was past dinner time, but I couldn't fathom the idea of food anyway. The peanuts the flight attendant had handed out hours ago were sitting like lead in my stomach.

Looking out the small window of the

airplane, seeing the ground rush up to meet me, I knew Ryan was right. My family would be happy to see me, and they would welcome me back with open arms, but I wasn't just nervous about that. Returning home meant I finally had to get help.

Was I ready for that?

The plane touched down and Ryan squeezed my hand once more.

Ready or not...

***

Ryan pulled his rental car into the driveway of my parents' home. I hadn't been here in more than four years, and it looked exactly the same. The two story colonial with snow white shingles and hunter green shutters was welcoming. It had always been a sanctuary for me...until nothing was.

The house held some of my fondest memories but also my saddest. Some of the dark days I couldn't even remember. The last time I was in that house, I sent Ryan away and later hurt myself. I still had no recollection of harming myself—I wasn't sure I wanted to remember.

"Are you ready?"

I stared through the windshield at what used to be my bedroom window and nodded. I was as ready as I was ever going to be.

"Good, because here they come," he nodded towards the house.

My eyes flashed to the front porch. My father stood in the doorway with my mother behind him. They looked concerned, probably wondering who was arriving unexpectedly at their house that late, since they wouldn't recognize the rental car.

Ryan opened his door and stepped out. My parents smiled when they saw him and started moving down the walkway to greet him. I took a deep breath and opened my door. The sound caught their attention, and they stopped walking as they looked over to where I was standing. My mother raised one hand to her mouth as her eyes widened in surprise.

"Anna?" she cried. "Is that really you, sweetie?"

I nodded, unable to find my voice and took a small, nervous step towards them. They looked between Ryan and me, as if they couldn't believe their eyes. Then suddenly, my mother laughed. She *laughed*, and then she was running. Once she reached me, she embraced me like she might never let me go.

"I can't believe it," she repeated, over and over again. "My baby girl is home."

She pulled away, framing my face in her hands and looking at me with absolute, unconditional love. I looked into her eyes—hazel eyes that matched mine—and took in her fine, delicate features. She had more lines around her eyes and a few grey hairs scattered throughout her blonde hair, but she was still beautiful.

"Happy birthday, sweet girl," she finally said.

My breath caught. It was my birthday. I'd forgotten. I hadn't celebrated the day in years, not since before the shooting. I looked over to Ryan, who was talking to my dad, and he gave me a small smile. Had he remembered it was my birthday?

"Come, come inside," my mother urged,

putting her arm around my shoulders and walking me towards the house. "Veronica was reading in bed. She's probably beside herself wondering what all the fuss is about. She'll be so happy to see you."

Just as I was about to walk through the front door, a heavy hand on my shoulder stopped me. I turned around to face my dad. He examined me, taking me in from head to toe, then he pulled me into his chest, cradling my head with his hand.

I relaxed into his hold, feeling safe and at home cradled in his warmth...and then I cried.

"It's okay," he said, rubbing my back with one hand, just like Ryan had. "Everything is going to be okay."

For the first time since I'd seen Ryan on the streets of Seattle, I believed everything really *would* be okay.

In the background, I could just barely hear my mother thanking Ryan for bringing me home.

"What is going on out there?" Ronnie's voice echoed in the front hall.

I pulled away from my dad and turned to my sister. She looked the same, maybe a little more mature, but still as gorgeous as ever. She had a different chair, which made sense since I doubted they lasted that long. This one looked fancier, and had cream colored vinyl with rose gold accents. Only the trendiest for my big sis. I was glad that hadn't changed.

"Anna?" Her mouth dropped and her face paled, as though she was looking at a ghost. In many ways, she was. I was a ghost of the person I had been years ago.

"Hey, Ronnie."

"You look like shit."

"Veronica!" Mom scolded, but I just laughed.

"It's good to see you, too." I dropped down to my knees, leaned across her legs, and hugged her. She held me back, squeezing a little too hard, but I'd never tell her.

"I missed you," she whispered. "I'm so glad you're home."

~ 4 ~

Anna

"I didn't think mom was ever going to let you go," Ronnie said as I laid beside her on her bed later that night.

"I didn't mind." It had been so long since I'd been hugged and doted on and loved that if my mother had asked me to sleep in her bed that night, in between her and my dad like I'd done as a child, I would have dove right between them.

"You're here to stay, right?"

"I think so."

"It will kill Mom and Dad if you take off again," she said, her voice firm and her words blunt. So very Ronnie.

"I want to stay," I told her truthfully.

"Good, because I missed my sister."

"I missed you, too." I rolled onto my side and grinned at her. It felt good to smile again. It felt great to be here with her like this.

My eyes scanned Ronnie. She looked good, real good. The years had been much kinder to her than they had to been to me. Of course, she was at home with a family who loved her, and she was taking care of herself. I'd been in the exact opposite position. All alone and broke, eating ramen noodles and drinking tap water. I couldn't remember the last time I'd eaten a vegetable.

"So you've been in Seattle all this time?" Ryan had shared with my family how he stumbled upon me. My mom nearly swooned, talking about fate and making Ryan and me both extremely uncomfortable. Was it fate that put Ryan and me on the same street at the same time? I didn't know. But if there was a force working for us that day, I appreciated it.

"I wandered around a little bit before ending up there."

"Any exciting adventures?" Ronnie asked, nestling into her pillow.

"Not a one."

"How did you end up in Seattle of all places? Couldn't get far enough away?" She joked, but her words were close to the truth. I had set out for the west coast to get as far away from Lakeside as I could.

"I took the train to Chicago and stayed there for a few months, then I hit Denver. I guess I didn't find what I was looking for in those places, so I kept heading west. Eventually I ended up in Seattle. I was out of money so I needed to find work. I just ended up staying there."

Ronnie scrunched up her nose. "Wasn't it cold? I think of those cities, and I think wind, snow, and rain."

"That was the appeal," I admitted.

"Cold, crappy weather?"

I nodded, then said, "I wanted to be numb. I didn't want to feel anything anymore."

Ronnie tugged on my arm, pulling my upper body over to her—the girl was strong!—and hugged me. I let her be the big sister and rested my head on her shoulder. I really, really missed her.

"I'm so sorry you felt that way." She began,

and I started to tell her it wasn't her fault, but she stopped me. "It's honest time, okay?" She waited until I nodded, then continued. "I'm sorry about our fight," she said, referring to the argument we'd had the night I got sent to Three Lakes.

"It's not your fault, Ronnie. You were only speaking the truth, I just didn't want to hear it. I was messed up...I still am. I shouldn't have reacted the way I did," I insisted, thinking back to that night.

"You need to get your shit together."

I rolled my eyes, not in the mood for Ronnie's shit.

"Don't roll your eyes at me, Anna. What you did to Ryan...that was bullshit. You know it, too, otherwise you wouldn't have been in here crying your eyes out ever since he left."

"What the hell do you know?" I snapped, hating that she knew I'd been crying. I stomped over to the mirror on my closet door. Taking in my reflection, I scowled. If my damp cheeks weren't enough of an indication, the puffy, red eyes gave it away.

"I know that you're miserable. You've been miserable for months. You're pushing everyone away from you, including Ryan. Mom and Dad are beside themselves, and Ryan...I've never seen him like that before," she finished in a quiet voice.

I looked at my sister, still as beautiful and put together as she was the day we went dress shopping. The bullet might have caused enough damage to her thoracic nerves to result in paralysis, but it sure didn't break her spirit.

Ronnie was a fighter.

She was kind, determined, and inspirational.

She was everything I wasn't.

"He was devastated, Anna."

I looked away, as if not seeing her would stop me from hearing her words.

"I get it, Anna. Ryan gets it, too. What happened to you—to us—was horrible...horrific. No one expects you to let it go, but you can't just stop living. You've done nothing the past six months but sit in your room and stare out that damn window. You need to get help—"

I shot my sister a glare as I laid down on my bed. "I'm not talking to a damn shrink again. That woman was crazier than I am."

"You can see another therapist, Anna," she said, rolling over to me. "Maybe Dr. Peters? She's been wonderful for me."

"No." I said the word with finality, but Ronnie ignored me.

"Yes. This is ridiculous," she slapped her hands against her lifeless legs, the sound causing me to startle. "Ryan's not going to wait forever for you to get your shit together. He already has the patience of a saint."

"I don't want him to wait," I argued, resting my head on my pillow and turning away from her.

"So what? You want him to meet another girl? Someone who will fall in love with his big biceps and rock hard abs...someone who will get to see him look all sexy in his uniform? Then he'll fall in love with her, too. They'll get married and have babies, and you'll be nothing but a memory," Ronnie said. I could hear her sneer. "A bad one. Because all he'll

think of when he thinks of you is how you threw him away like a piece of trash even though he put his life on hold for you, over and over—"

"Shut up!" I screamed, sitting straight up and pulling my knees into my chest. "Shut up, shut up, shut up!" I pulled at my hair, rocking back and forth, as tears streamed down my face, screaming those two words over and over again.

I was vaguely aware of my sister rolling away from my bed, calling for my mom.

I heard my parents' voices, but they sounded so far away.

Ronnie apologized, "I'm so sorry, Anna," over and over again.

Then everything went black.

"Ever since the shooting, I've felt so incredibly guilty," Ronnie whispered, bringing me back to the present.

"Why?" I asked, wondering if I'd missed something while I was lost in my memory. "You didn't pull the trigger. You got shot, for crying out loud."

"I know, that's not why I felt guilty," she paused, and I heard a sniffle. "I felt guilty because I bounced back. I thought that maybe there was something wrong with me, you know? Why wasn't I as messed up about it as you were? I was the one who was shot. I worried that maybe you were holding the weight for both of us, and I felt so horrible about that."

I picked up my head and looked her in the eyes. "You know that's not how it was."

She nodded and wiped the tears from her

cheeks. "I know that now. My therapist helped me understand how people can respond to the same situation differently. She reminded me that while I may have gotten injured physically, you...you saw stuff...that probably affected you emotionally."

The barista. Blood spatter. Tears. More gun shots. Glass breaking.

"I see her every time I close my eyes. Every time," I confessed, my eyes welling up. It was the first time I'd said the words aloud, and the next breath I took felt lighter, like a small weight was lifted off my chest.

"You should to talk to someone," Ronnie suggested quietly.

"I know."

"I bet Dr. Matson will still see you...the one that got away," she added wistfully.

I laughed. God, I missed Ronnie and her weird sense of humor.

"I did like her," I said, thinking fondly of the doctor I'd seen when I'd spent a few months at an adolescent treatment facility after having a breakdown that night with Ronnie. "But I'm twenty-two now. She might not see me since I'm not an adolescent."

"Oh, pish posh. She'll see you," she said. I could hear the smile in her voice. She was always happiest when she was getting things done and making plans. "We'll have Mom make you an appointment with Dr. Matson tomorrow."

"We?"

She nudged my head with her shoulder, making it bounce. I giggled, the sound foreign to my ears. "Yes, 'we.' You're not alone anymore, Anna."

Something warm and fuzzy settled over me at her statement. *I wasn't alone anymore.* The idea of being part of something again—a family—made me feel like I could do anything.

"So tell me about Ryan," Ronnie asked, breaking the heavy moment with her suggestive tone.

"There's nothing to tell."

"Oh, come on. There's got to be something; he swooped in and saved you like a white knight. Any old feelings still there?"

"It's been a long time, Ronnie. I'm sure he's moved on by now," I said, ignoring her question and the tingles that spread throughout my body.

Did I still have feelings for Ryan? I was sure I always would. He was my first boyfriend, first kiss, first love, first...everything. He'd always hold a special place in my heart. But I wasn't sure if I still had *feelings* for him.

"That wasn't what I asked." She was so persistent.

"I'll always love him because our time together was so special, but what we had is broken. I broke it."

"Don't sell yourself short. He called here all the time when you were gone, checking to see if we'd heard from you. If we did hear from you, he asked what you said."

"He told me," I said, remembering our conversation at the hotel.

"I think he still cares," Ronnie yawned.

I had no doubt that Ryan still cared. He wouldn't have dropped his plans—important ones, at that—and brought me home if he didn't care. But everything was different now.

"It doesn't matter. I need to focus on getting my head straight. I can't get involved with anyone."

"That's very mature of you," Ronnie agreed.

"So what about you? Any guys catching my big sister's interest lately?"

Ronnie's high school boyfriend, Derek, had dumped her when he realized her wheelchair wouldn't fit into their golden couple image. He was a douche with a capital D. Ronnie was all torn up about it at the time, but it's been a while, and she may have found someone new. I had so much to catch up on.

"Oh! There's this guy in my abnormal psych class who is so hot," Ronnie said excitedly. She proceeded to tell me all about Dave from class, and what a sweet and funny guy he was.

Closing my eyes, I listened to her go on and on about Dave. I was happy for my sister, but I couldn't stop my mind from wandering to the guy with eyes the color of the midnight sky.

Did he still have feelings for me?

Did he love me?

Would I ever be able to right the wrong I'd done to him?

Only time would tell.

~ 5 ~

Ryan

Getting to be part of Anna's reunion with her family was a gratifying experience and not because I'd helped facilitate it. Seeing the joy on the faces of four people who'd been so hurt was something I'd never forget.

Though I'd kept in touch with the Romano family, I hadn't been inside the house since the day Anna had thrown me out and broken my heart.

"Is today a good day or a bad day?" I quietly asked Mrs. Romano as we stood outside Anna's bedroom door. Six months had passed since the shooting, and Anna grew more and more withdrawn every day. There were days when I visited that she didn't speak at all. Those days were increasing in frequency.

"Every day is a bad day, Ryan," Anna's mom sighed. The past six months had aged her. She looked exhausted, and I knew she and Mr. Romano were at a loss for what to do. Anna refused to go to therapy...she refused to talk to anyone, including me.

"I have to leave," I told her, choking on the agony of leaving Anna and moving on with my life without her. We were supposed to take this step together. Separate, but together. It was why I'd waited a year after I graduated high school to enlist. We were supposed to leave

Lakeside together, then reunite wherever I was after she finished college.

Best laid plans...

"I know you do, sweetie." Mrs. Romano gave me a sympathetic smile and patted my arm. "I'll give the two of you some time."

I watched her retreating back as she went down the stairs, her shoes making light clicks as they met each step. I was going to miss the Romanos. They'd been like a second family to me, especially since my parents were constantly out of town traveling for work.

Once Mrs. Romano was out of sight, I pushed open Anna's bedroom door. She sat on the window seat like she did every day, staring out at nothing. It used to be her favorite place, but I wasn't sure what it was for her anymore since she didn't seem to experience any pleasure these days.

I approached her quietly, but the sudden stiffness in her posture let me know she was aware of my presence. She could feel me the way I felt her. I never needed to touch her to know she was near. We were always that connected, since the moment we met in art class on my first day at Lakeside High. It reassured me that even though we were as far apart as two people could be while in the same room together, we were still close.

I pressed a kiss onto the top of her head, running a hand through her long, soft hair. She didn't exactly welcome the action, but she didn't flinch either. I crouched down beside her, giving her the higher position in case she felt she needed it. I didn't know what she needed anymore, and it gutted me. I hated not being able to support her; it made me feel like less of a man, even though I wasn't yet nineteen.

"Hey, baby," I greeted her. No reaction. "Can you look at me, Anna?" My voice was soft and pleading, but, again, it had no effect. "I'm leaving tomorrow," I said finally.

Anna said nothing. She still didn't move. She just kept looking out that window, as if lost in her own little world. I was worried sick about her, and as much as I wanted to stay by her side and try to push her to get better, I couldn't put off my future any longer.

"I don't know what to do here, A," I said, using the nickname I had for her, hoping for a reaction.

I finally got one.

Turning her head slowly, she looked me in the eyes for the first time in months. I didn't like what I saw. She looked empty, like she was completely dead inside. Those eyes that used to spark with life were glazed over, as if she were high. I'd consider that a possibility if not for the fact that she never, ever left her room and didn't have any visitors. Her family would never slip her anything, either, and I knew for a fact that they started locking up all the medicine in the house at the suggestion of Anna's counselor—the counselor she spent all of twenty minutes with before calling bullshit and never returning. No, Anna's problems were all inside her mind.

"Just go," she whispered coolly, her voice emotionless.

My eyes widened, and I reached a hand up to touch her face, but she turned back towards the window before I made contact. I dropped my hand as disappointment rushed over me

39

like a tidal wave. I felt like I was drowning...I couldn't breathe.

Looking down at her royal blue carpet, I spoke softly, letting it all out one last time. "I love you, Anna. I want you to be better. I hate that I can't fix this for you. I hate that no one can. I wish there was something we could have done differently that day. I miss you. I know that's so fucking selfish of me, but I miss you. I miss the way things were. I wish we could go back..." I trailed off, doubting she was even listening to me. "I'm leaving tomorrow."

This was a moment we should have been celebrating. It was supposed to be the first day of the rest of our lives, the day we started our dreams. She was supposed to be leaving for art school in San Diego, and I was entering the Navy. We'd say goodbye, and it would suck, but we'd do it with the promise of seeing each other again soon, as better versions of ourselves. Instead, I was sad, missing my girlfriend of three years who was sitting right in front of me. She was the love of my life, and she was breaking my heart.

"Go," she said again, her voice more firm than I'd heard in weeks.

"Baby—"

"Just go, Ryan. I don't want you here."

Dejected, I left her bedroom and I left her; my broken heart barely beating in my chest.

After saying goodbye to her parents and to Ronnie, I left her house that day and never went back. I'd kept in touch, but I couldn't go there, especially after she took off. I rarely returned to Lakeside at all after I enlisted. My parents' travel schedule tended to clash with my leave, so more often than not, they ended up visiting me wherever I was instead of me going home to an empty house in a town full of memories I yearned to forget.

As I lay in my childhood bedroom—complete with posters of Victoria's Secret models I couldn't remember the names of, memorabilia from my favorite sport teams, and trophies and awards from my major accomplishments—I thought briefly about what could have been.

Anna would have been through with college by now, so we'd probably be living together, or at least in the same city. She'd be sketching or maybe even painting, if she'd honed her skills with the brushes in art school the way she'd always hoped. Without a doubt, I knew we'd have been happy.

My phone buzzed with an incoming Facetime call, interrupting my musings. *Kelsey.* As much as I didn't want to face the present, I knew I had to answer since it was our usual time to talk. I tapped the green circle.

"Hey, princess."

~ **6** ~

Anna

Ronnie was right, Dr. Matson cleared her schedule to see me. Surprised to hear from my mother, she'd wanted to see me as soon as possible. That's how I found myself sitting in her office the day after I'd returned home.

I was surprised to discover that Dr. Matson had an office outside of Three Lakes—the adolescent mental health facility I spent a short three and a half months in. Located off the main strip in downtown Lakeside, her office was inside a small converted house. The kitchen and dining room were made into a waiting area, and I guessed the bedrooms were offices or meeting rooms, but I hadn't been down that hallway yet.

Mom and I sat on one of the overstuffed couches in the waiting area. Designed to be comfortable with its soft furniture and soothing with its pale colors, the room made me feel like I was making the right decision being there.

I stood from the couch and walked over to the wall, looking at one of the paintings, an abstract design in vibrant colors. Several of them dotted the walls in the room. I briefly recalled the various pieces of art in the hallways of Three Lakes. Residents in art therapy had proudly displayed their projects on the walls, and I wondered if any of the pieces here were from former patients of Dr.

Matson.

"Anna?" a woman called from behind me. The familiar voice sent me back in time.

When I came to, I was in a ten by ten white room with fluorescent lights fitted into the drop ceiling.

"Good morning, Annalise," a warm, yet unfamiliar, voice said.

I rolled my head to the side and spotted a woman in a white lab coat sitting on a stool in the far corner of the room. She looked to be about my mother's age, mid-forties, with dark brown hair and dark eyes. She wore gray slacks and a pale pink blouse under her coat.

"Anna," I corrected her use of my full name. I never went by Annalise, it was so formal. "Where am I?" I asked her, though I already knew...not my exact location, but that I was in some kind of hospital.

"Sorry, Anna," she amended, smiling kindly at me. "You're at Three Lakes. It's a residential treatment facility for adolescents, like yourself, who are going through some difficult times in their lives. I'm Dr. Matson."

"I don't want to be here," I said defiantly, letting the doctor know up front that I wasn't going to cooperate with whatever plan she and my parents had concocted.

"I realize that, and I hope you change your mind. In the meantime, you're going to have to stay. At least for the next three and a half months or sooner if you get better."

Three and a half months...I turned eighteen in three and a half months.

"Where are my parents?" A tear escaped the corner of my eye and I tried to lift a hand

to swipe at it, but I couldn't move my arms. Brown leather straps constrained each of my wrists, keeping them down by my sides. "Why am I tied up?" I asked. My heart was beginning to beat a punishing rhythm in my chest. It hurt to breathe.

"Do you remember what happened last night?" Dr. Matson asked, tilting her head to the side.

Digging into the deep recesses of my mind, I couldn't recall anything since...since Ryan left. Since I sent him away. More tears spilled from my eyes, rolling down my temples and into my hair.

"You remember something?" Dr. Matson asked.

"Ryan," I whispered.

She looked at her notepad. "He's your boyfriend?"

"Was."

"You broke up?"

"Yes."

"Do you remember what happened after he left?"

I remembered crying. Then Ronnie. Ronnie was in my room. She was telling me all sorts of things I didn't want to hear about Ryan. About him finding someone else, loving her, getting married and having babies. I remember telling her to shut up. Then there was yelling...it was me...I was yelling. Then nothing.

"You hurt yourself pretty bad, Anna," Dr. Matson said, rising from her stool and walking over to my bedside. She had a mirror in her right hand, the kind a hairdresser would use to show you the back of your hairstyle. I eyed

the mirror, scared of what she was going to show me. "You scratched your face," she told me softly, raising the mirror so I could see. "Do you remember that?"

I looked into the mirror and my eyes widened as I took in the red scratches all over my face. Some had bled and were beginning to scab over, but others were just angry and raw looking scrapes.

I looked away and shook my head to answer the doctor's question. I didn't remember doing that. I didn't remember it at all. Oddly, I believed that I'd done it anyway.

Dr. Matson lowered the mirror. "We're here to help you, Anna, not hinder you. Your mother and father love you very much. They want what's best for you. Veronica, too. If you work with us, if you make a commitment to get better, you'll be back home in no time."

I moved my eyes to the ceiling, focusing on a small water stain on the ceiling tile next to the air vent, and started my countdown. Three and a half months...

"Anna...honey?" Mom's concerned voice startled me.

"Sorry," I said, moving to smile at her and Dr. Matson. "I was just remembering the first time we met."

"It's good to see you," Dr. Matson said, stepping forward and putting out her hand. I shook it, and she and Mom shared a quick hug. *Hm, they seemed close.* "Grace, it's good to see you as well. Let's go back."

We followed Dr. Matson down the short hallway and into a small room with rose wallpaper and more paintings.

"Are these from one of your patients?" I asked, gesturing towards the two red, abstract paintings that matched the color of the roses on the walls. I didn't know how I knew they were by the same artist, I just did.

"They are," Dr. Matson answered, standing beside me. "Do you like them?"

I tilted my head, studying the side-by-side paintings. I hadn't really looked at a painting in years...since *before*. I tried to see what the artist saw, but I was at a loss.

"They're interesting," I finally said.

"I agree. Why don't we all take a seat?"

Doing as I was told, I sat on the cream colored sofa beside my mother. Taking my hand in hers, she leant her support. She was pleased when Ronnie had told her of my interest in seeing Dr. Matson again, and I didn't want to disappoint her. Dr. Matson sat in a crimson armchair across from us.

"So, Anna, let's talk about why you're here."

Mom squeezed my hand, giving me the encouragement I needed. "I'm ready for a change," I said, then added, "I need to change."

"Tell me what you'd like to do, how you'd like to be."

I blew out a breath. Dr. Matson wasn't going to make it easy for me; I knew that from my time at Three Lakes. She wouldn't give me the answers; she would make me come up with them.

"I want to live again...really live. Ever since the...shooting," the word still so hard to say, "I've been trying to stay numb. I haven't wanted to feel anything."

"Why do you think that is?"

"Because if I didn't feel anything, then I wouldn't be scared. I wouldn't hurt for the people who lost their lives that day at the mall. For weeks, all I could think about was them. Images of the victims I'd seen that day flashed through my mind every day. The father and son from the play area who lost their wife and mother, the barista...every time I close my eyes I see her face."

"You were close to the events," she observed.

Even though I'd seen Dr. Matson at Three Lakes, I never spoke to her. I never contributed to group or individual counseling sessions. Dr. Matson knew nothing of me. She knew nothing of the incident that had changed my life, except what everyone had learned in the news.

"So close," I confessed. "I was sitting right outside the coffee shop when he started shooting inside. I...I looked right at her, his girlfriend, right before she died." My mother gasped, I'd never spoken of that day to anyone, so she had no clue just how close I'd been to it all. "She looked so scared. She was so scared and I...I ran away."

"It seems like you feel some guilt," Dr. Matson said.

"Yeah...I guess I do," I agreed, realizing it for the first time myself.

"While there was absolutely nothing normal about what you experienced that day, it is normal to feel some guilt as a result. There are always what ifs. What if I had done this? What if I had done that? But Anna, in your case, if you had done something, then he might have taken your life, too."

I nodded, knowing she was right. Being more than a bystander that day could have killed me—it had killed others at the mall that day. Imagine if I had tried to stop or distract him?

"Sometimes I wonder why I was spared," I said, voicing another unspoken thought. "Seven people died, Ronnie got shot, and I was sitting right there and nothing happened to me. The guy had to have walked right by me. I just don't understand."

"You probably never will, Anna. It's not something you can understand. He was a very sick man."

"I was so naïve. Before that day, I'd heard the stories and read the news reports of shootings, but I never thought something like that would happen in my town, let alone in such close proximity to me. I was a happy-go-lucky teenager with nothing on my mind but my next school assignment and what the weekend would bring. In one moment, all of that was taken away from me."

"You were scared."

"I still am," I admitted quietly, a tear running down my cheek.

"Let's talk about what scares you."

"Everything. Life, death...strangers, crowds..." I trailed off.

"You've been away from home for a while now, on your own...how have you dealt with that?"

"I kept to myself. Anywhere I went, I looked for all the exits so I would know all the ways out if I needed to escape."

"It must have been pretty lonely being by

yourself for four years."

"I didn't let myself feel," I shrugged. "I stayed numb."

"Tell me about this numbness," Dr. Matson probed, and I knew what she was getting at. She wanted to know if I used drugs or alcohol to numb myself.

"I didn't use drugs, and I didn't drink," I told her. What I didn't say was that I probably would have used had I been able to afford the habit.

The rest of the session was spent with me talking about what my life was like while I was away from Lakeside, and the myriad of emotions I'd felt over the years. I could tell some of it was difficult for my mother to hear, but I was glad she was there with me. I felt a little more relaxed with my mom by my side. Grace Romano was fiercely supportive of her children, and perhaps, for the first time in my life, I appreciated that quality.

"Okay, Anna. I think we've had a great start here today. I'd like to see you again, same time next week. Is that okay?"

"Yes." It wasn't like I had anything else to do, but in all honestly, I enjoyed talking with Dr. Matson. If I wanted to get better, I knew I had to make an effort.

"Good," she nodded, scribbling a note on a pad she'd pulled from the table beside her chair. "I'm giving you some homework this week. I'd like for you to make a list of some of the activities you enjoyed doing before the shooting. Can you do that for me?" I nodded, and she continued. "I'd also like for you to make a list of any goals you used to have."

"Okay," I agreed.

"Great," she smiled, standing up. Mom and I stood as well. "It's not going to be easy, but we're going to work through this, okay?"

"Yes," Something that felt an awful lot like optimism began to rise in my chest.

"I'll see you next week, Anna. If you don't mind, I'd like to talk to your mom for a minute before you go."

"Of course," I said, giving my mom a smile to let her know I was okay. With a small wave to Dr. Matson, I slipped out the door.

~ 7 ~

Anna

Silence echoed throughout the car as Mom drove us home from my first therapy session. She hadn't said a word, aside from asking me if I was ready to go, since she stepped out of Dr. Matson's office. I didn't know what was plaguing her, but I imagined it had to do with what I talked about during the session.

She pulled her Mercedes into the driveway, pausing only to wait for the garage door to rise, then parked inside.

"I won't be sitting in on your future sessions," she said finally, taking the key out of the ignition.

"Why not?"

She fiddled with the keys in her hand, the clanking of the metal the only sound in the car. "Dr. Matson thinks it would be best for you to have one-on-one sessions with her. Said your father and I might be a distraction."

"That's not true," I argued. I wasn't sure I was ready to talk to my therapist without the strength of my mother beside me.

"You may be less willing to talk about some things in our presence, and that's understandable, Anna. You're a grown woman. You can attend therapy without your parents," she gave me a soft smile. "If you ever want us there, just say the word, but I think Dr. Matson is right. I think you need this time with her to heal, and we may hinder

51

your progress if you hold things back because we're listening."

"I guess I understand that." Sort of. Not really. I really wanted my mom.

"I...I had no idea, no idea what you went through that day. You never talked about it. Veronica and Ryan told us what they saw, but I'm not even sure they realized just how close you were to it all. I knew we could have lost you, you and Ronnie and Ryan, but I didn't realize just how close we'd come to that. Today was a surprise. I don't want to dwell on the past, I want us all to be able to move forward. I want to help you move forward. I just had no idea, and it startled me to hear it."

I turned towards her, placing my hand on her arm. "It's okay, Mom. I should have talked about it a long time ago. I'm—" I choked up.

"It's okay, Anna."

"No...it's not okay. I'm sorry, Mom. I'm sorry for what I put you and Dad through. Ronnie, too. I'm sorry I upset you all, and I'm sorry I scared you. I was just so scared myself. I didn't know how to process what I was feeling. I'm still not sure how to."

Tears trailed down my face, and she used her thumbs to wipe them away. Still holding my face, she smiled at me and said "We're going to help you get through this, Anna. You weren't ready before, but you're ready now."

"I am ready," I agreed with a sniffle.

"Good," she said, dropping her hands and gathering her bag. "Now, how about we go inside and bake something?"

"That sounds fantastic," I grinned. It felt

like forever since I baked something with my mom.

"I'm proud of you, Anna," Mom said with a quick smile, then she got out of the car and went into the house.

I followed behind, reflecting on my session with Dr. Matson and thinking about the lists she'd asked me to make. Art was the biggest thing. It would be on the top of both lists— something I used to enjoy doing and a goal I wanted to set for myself. I wanted to start sketching again, and I wanted to get back on track for art school. I only hoped I still had what it would take to get there.

"Hey, Ron," I greeted my sister as I stepped through the garage door into the kitchen.

"Hey, Ryan came looking for you while you were out."

"Oh?" My heart started beating a little bit faster at the sound of his name. "Did he say why?"

"He wanted to say goodbye."

"He left?" I asked, my face falling.

Ronnie nodded, giving me a sad smile. "He left this for you," she said, rolling over to me and handing me a small folded up piece of paper.

"Did you read it?" I asked, though I wasn't sure why. I knew she'd respect my privacy. Even if Ryan and I weren't anything anymore, we were a thing once, and that meant something between sisters.

"Of course not," Ronnie said, giving me a sour look.

"I know. I'm sorry." I looked over to my mom, who had been silently watching our exchange. "Can you give me a few minutes, then I'll be down to bake?"

"Sure, sweetie. Take your time."

Thanking her and promising I'd be right back, I ran up to my room, leaving her and Ronnie in the kitchen discussing what sweet treat to make. I shut my bedroom door behind me and flopped down on my bed, resting my upper body on my elbows, the small piece of paper clutched in my hand.

Upset over missing him, I was disappointed I hadn't spent more time with Ryan before he had to go. I knew he wouldn't have been able to stay here forever. I never even asked when he had to go back. I would have liked to have been able to say goodbye, to thank him for getting me home.

I unfolded the piece of paper, and frowned at the few short lines of text on the page.

Anna,
Sorry I missed you.
I'm glad you're home,
and I hope you find what
you're looking for.
Keep in touch.
Ryan

It was the most impersonal five lines I'd ever read. I'd seen Craigslist ads with more emotion than his note. We weren't anything anymore, though. He didn't owe me an eloquent message after I'd broken his heart. I deserved much less than even this...but it still hurt. We'd been through so many epic moments together. Ryan was once my everything. He was there on the worst day of my life, and he saved me. He saved me again a few days ago on a random street in a random city and brought me home. He had more feelings inside him than this measly note. At least he left his email address.

Keep in touch.

That was what people wrote in the yearbooks of classmates they didn't intend to speak to after graduation. Did he really want me to keep in touch? Or was he just saying that to be nice? Nothing about his little note shouted at me to keep in touch.

Reaching over, I opened the drawer of my nightstand—packed full of stuff I'd sift through later—and dropped the note on top. Closing the drawer, I rolled over and sat up.

This wasn't the time to overanalyze Ryan's note. This was the time to bake.

"Anna!" As if she had been cued, Ronnie's voice rang up the stairs, right through my closed door.

"I'm coming!" I yelled back.

Taking one last look at my nightstand, I got up from my bed and left the room.

Later.

I'd overanalyze later.

In the kitchen, Ronnie was propped up on a chair-back stool at the island. It was rigged with some sort of seatbelt attachment so she wouldn't fall off. In front of her was a mixing bowl and various ingredients. Mom was shuffling around the kitchen, pulling measuring spoons and cups out of drawers and cabinets.

"Can you grab me a rubber spatula?" Ronnie asked me as I stepped in the room. Swiping one out of the vase-like utensil holder on the counter by the oven, I tossed it over to her, and she caught it with a grin.

"Pre-heat the oven to three-fifty," Mom called out, now hovering over a recipe card. I did as asked, then hopped up on the stool beside Ronnie.

"What are we making?"

"White chocolate chip cookies," Ronnie smirked.

My favorite.

~ 8 ~

Anna

"At the end of our last session, I asked you to come up with a list of activities you used to enjoy and some goals. Have you done that?" Dr. Matson was all business this session.

"I did."

"Good," she said, her white teeth glimmering behind her smile. "Care to share them with me?"

This was the first step to getting better, trusting Dr. Matson and her processes. Taking a deep breath, I began. "I used to sketch," I said, addressing the first item.

"Your parents said you were very good," she commented, and I nodded.

It was no secret that I had been a good artist. My work was often featured in showcases at my high school. It wasn't about conceit, either. As an artist, any kind of artist really, you had to have some level of confidence in your work. How else could you expect the public to?

"What else do you have?"

"I used to hike and sometimes jog." Though the jogging was more Ryan's thing. He had always been very athletic, and when he decided to join the military, he amped up his exercise.

"Good."

"And reading. That's the last thing," I finished, dropping the torn piece of notebook paper onto my lap.

"These are all good activities, Anna. Have you tried engaging in any of them since the incident?" Dr. Matson didn't say (or use) the word "shooting" to describe that day; instead, she referred to it as the "event" or "incident," or something of the like. I wasn't sure why that was, but I appreciated not hearing it. I think she knew that.

"Not unless running to the bus stop counts as jogging."

She chuckled, making a note on her pad. "I think not. How about your goals?"

"College," I answered quickly, wanting to ignore the rest of my list.

"You wanted to go to Braddock Art Institute before, right?"

"They have an excellent art program."

"It's probably very competitive."

"Yeah, most serious art schools are."

"You haven't drawn in years, and you have to finish high school."

"I know," I said, looking down at the dumb little piece of parchment holding all my hopes and dreams. Hopes and dreams I thought, until just a moment ago, were still within my grasp.

"I'm not trying to discourage you, Anna. I'm just reminding you that you need to crawl before you walk. Each goal needs to be broken down into smaller goals. Steps, if you will. We'll get back to art school in just a minute. What else is on your list?"

I looked at the next three words scribbled on the paper.

Mom

Dad
Ronnie

"I want to make amends with my family." It was mostly the truth.

"Tell me more about what you want to do there."

Shifting on the sofa, I sighed. This was harder than I thought it would be. "I want to earn back their trust. I don't want them to worry about me anymore. I want to...to apologize for making them worry before. For scaring them and for leaving. I was...awful. I didn't take them into consideration at all..."

"You're feeling some guilt?"

"Yes. I'm feeling a lot of guilt where they're concerned."

"And alleviating that guilt will make you feel better about you?"

"I think so."

"Good. I just want to make sure you're choosing goals that will benefit you in the long run. I don't want you to focus so much of your energy on other people, and not enough on yourself. If the end result of making amends with your family is a positive one for you, then I support that."

"Aren't you supposed to support my choices no matter what?" I asked, quirking my lip as I remembered something that was said in group therapy at Three Lakes. I might not have participated, but I listened.

Dr. Matson smirked back. "You're too smart for your own good. How about I be the therapist and you be the client, hmm?"

I glance at my lap to hide my smile. "Deal."

"Good. What else do you have on your

goals list?"

Eyeing the last item on the list, I hesitated.

Dr. Matson noticed. "This one seems a bit more difficult for you."

"It is difficult," I admitted.

"Tell me about it."

"The day I was admitted to Three Lakes, I broke up with my boyfriend."

"Ryan."

"Yeah. We dated for almost four years. He was there...that day," I didn't need to tell her what day I was referring to. "He was also with me afterwards. Every day. I was awful to him. Really, truly awful. I broke up with him. Broke his heart." And subsequently lost my mind.

"More guilt," Dr. Matson observed.

"Yeah," I said, wiping a tear from my eye. "I broke his heart and, when I bumped into him in Seattle—of all places—he was still so kind to me. I felt like the worst kind of human being. I'm sure he's moved on, and I don't expect anything romantic to happen between us, but I need to make amends with Ryan, too. I also need to thank him, for everything he did for me. He probably saved my life the day of the shooting, and he saved me again in Washington."

"And if something romantic were to happen? You two have a history."

"I'm not ready for that." I meant the words as much then as I did when I'd said them to Ronnie.

"That's very mature thinking."

"I need to get better. I'm not really my own biggest fan right about now, so how can I expect someone else to be? I just really want to feel normal again. Whatever normal is."

She smiled. "We're going to work very hard to get you there."

I hoped so.

Hope.

It was all I had left.

***

Back at home that night, I laid on my bed, propped up on my elbows, with my sketchpad resting on my bent knees.

Dr. Matson and I had talked for the rest of our hour about how my activities could help support my goals. She suggested that engaging in my previous happy activities could provide assurance to my family that I was doing better and making an effort to change, which would assist in making amends. Then there was the obvious connection between drawing and college. We sort of left the topic of Ryan alone. He was gone, so it wasn't like he was something that needed to be addressed immediately. Except that while he wasn't physically present...he was mentally present.

I couldn't get him out of my head.

I started to scribble lines and circles on the paper, knowing that I just had to put the pencil to the paper to start creating *something*. It didn't even matter what it was, I needed to feel the familiar movement of pencil against paper...the light friction of graphite against parchment...the quiet scratching.

I imagined Ryan's dark blue eyes, and the way they appeared to shine when he looked at me—but only when he looked at *me*. The same applied to his smile. He had one smile, where the left side of his perfect lips quirked

61

up slightly higher than the right, that he only gave to me. Memories flowed through my mind of those eyes and that smile, and I recalled never feeling more loved than I had when *he* looked at me.

He was once my everything.

And I was his.

Shaking my head to clear it, I focused on the paper before me. My eyes widened in surprise at what was on it. I'd sketched him. *Ryan.* The dark, shiny eyes and crooked smile, perfect nose, and the sharp angles of his face. I'd captured it so well—like a photograph—and I wasn't even paying attention.

~ 9 ~

Anna

My mother volunteered at a soup kitchen two days a week. I went with her one Friday, with the promise we'd go Christmas shopping afterwards. It seemed contradictory to me, serving at a soup kitchen, then spending an exorbitant amount of money on frivolous gifts. That, however, didn't stop me.

Honestly, I wasn't interested in the gift shopping part of the day, I just wanted to go to the craft store so I could get some new paper, pencils, and charcoals. Mom and Dad were so thrilled I was expressing an interest in art again, they probably would have bought me the entire store if I'd asked.

Serving corn and green beans to the guests at the soup kitchen put a smile on my face. I made an effort to make conversation when I could, knowing I was nearly in the same position back in Seattle. There were times I could barely afford the ramen noodles that were a staple of my diet. Working at the soup kitchen made me realize exactly what I had...exactly what I had taken advantage of by taking off.

I should have sought help a long time ago.

I should never have left home.

I should have

I should

I

"You about ready?" Mom asked, startling

me. Nodding to her, I quickly rinsed the soap suds off the pot I'd been scrubbing and set it on the drying rack.

"Thanks, Grace. Nice to meet you, Anna," the outreach director called from across the room as Mom and I gathered our things. The nice older woman was cleaning the stainless steel counters of the facility's commercial kitchen.

"Nice to meet you, as well," I said as I took my coat and purse from my mother's outstretched hands.

"See you on Tuesday, Claire," Mom said as we left the kitchen. "How did you like helping out today?" she asked once we were outside.

I fastened the large buttons on my pea coat to ward off the December chill before answering her. "It really made me appreciate what I have."

She looked at me with admiration in her eyes, and I had to look away before I teared up. "I'm proud of you, Anna. You haven't been home a full week yet, but you've already made so many improvements."

"I'm trying really hard."

"I know," she said, putting her arm around my shoulder and pulling me into her side. "I know you are. I just wanted you to know that we've noticed. You're not the same girl you were when you left here years ago. Maybe one day you can tell me about your time away, but I won't force you to."

"I'd like that," I whispered. "Someday."

"It's a date." When we reached the car, she gave me one last squeeze and kissed the side of my head. "Let's shop!"

***

Mom had the foresight not to choose the Lakeside Mall for our shopping spree, instead we went to the small outlet center on the edge of town. It had fewer stores, but there were still plenty to choose from. An added bonus was that the craft store was in the same plaza.

While she shopped for gifts in the outlet shops, I meandered the craft store and filled a cart with art supplies. My new supplies inspired and motivated me, and the moment we arrived home, I hurried up to my bedroom and sketched. I spent hours pulling images from my memory bank and drawing them: the spring flowers from my mom's garden, Ronnie tipping her head back in laughter, and the old treehouse in Ryan's backyard. I had many fond memories of that treehouse.

Setting my pad to the side, I peered over at my nightstand, picturing the scrap of paper tucked inside.

I wanted to talk to Ryan. Was that selfish? He'd moved on with his life, and appeared to be doing well for himself. He looked good and healthy. *Would it be so terrible for me to reach out to him?* He told me to keep in touch...did he mean it?

Hopping off my bed, I went to my desk and powered up my old laptop, hoping it still worked. My room had been left untouched, so I imagined it would. I knew laptops didn't last forever though, and mine had already been a few years old before I left. The log-in screen came up, and I pumped my fist in the air as I took a seat on the wooden desk chair. *Success!* I typed in my password, *Ryan_0905*, smiling as I recalled the September day we'd first met. A day that changed my life.

Opening the internet browser, I pulled up my email account. I clicked to compose a new email, then got up and grabbed the folded piece of paper from its hiding place in my nightstand. Sitting down again, I began.

To: Ryan Jacobs
From: Anna Romano
Subject: Hello

Dear Ryan,
I have so much to say to you and I don't know where to begin, but first, I'd like to send you something, so if you have a mailing address you'd be willing to share, I would appreciate it.

Now that that's out of the way, I want to thank you. Thank you for bringing me home. I've felt more in the last week than I have in almost five years. I'm in therapy. I've only had two sessions so far, but I think I'm making progress already. I feel. I haven't allowed myself to feel since that day. It hurt too much.

I also need to apologize to you, Ryan. I was such a mess, and you suffered as a result of that. I'm sorry I closed myself off and ended up hurting you. I can't say it wasn't my intention because—sadly—I think it was. I wanted to push you away. I wanted to push my family away, too. I don't think it was because I didn't care about you, I think I knew I was all wrong inside. I think I was trying to be noble or something. I know

66

what you're thinking, it was a pretty shitty way to be noble. I agree with that now. But at the time...I just wasn't right. I'm still not right. I have a lot to work on, but I am working on it. I want to be better. I don't want to be scared and upset anymore. I want to be the person you all remember. A version of myself I can be proud of. Mom told me she was proud of me today. I appreciated it so much, but afterwards I kind of wondered how someone could be proud of me when I wasn't proud of myself. Kind of like how people say you can't love someone else until you love yourself. I don't know. It's probably just a mom thing, you know? They're supposed to love you unconditionally and all that. Maybe she sees something in me I don't see in myself.

I'm rambling. I'm sorry. Even after all these years, you're still so easy to talk to. I hope you're doing well, Ryan. I hope you're happy. I hope the Navy is as fulfilling as you'd always hoped. I'm so proud of you for achieving your dream. Thank you for being there for me, even when I made it difficult. I'm sorry for so much and want you to know that I appreciate you...more than you'll ever know.

Take care,
Anna

I pressed "send" without re-reading the message, not wanting to give myself the opportunity to second guess any of my words. I wanted Ryan to see it all...raw and uncut.

Now I hoped he'd write me back.

~ **10** ~

Ryan

Letting the searing hot water of the shower spray on my tense shoulders, I thanked my lucky stars I didn't screw up during the training exercises I'd participated in earlier that day. My mind wasn't right—it wasn't clear.

I couldn't stop thinking about Anna.

In my line of work, air traffic control, you couldn't have off days. You couldn't even have off seconds, and I'd been a mess out there.

I turned off the water and dried off with a towel, wrapping it around my waist when I finished. Exiting the bathroom, I walked to the kitchen of the off-base apartment I shared with one of my shipmates, Keith Rogers. After grabbing a bottle of water from the fridge, I went to my room to check my email. I checked it three times a day, every day, since I left Lakeside, hoping Anna had sent me a message.

There was never a message and the disappointment I felt...well, it was inappropriate. I shouldn't have been so damn eager to hear from her. I should have let that chapter of my life close.

While my computer booted up, I got dressed in a pair of workout shorts and a t-shirt. Rogers would probably want to hit the gym when he got off duty. The guy loved to workout. I didn't mind, working out was how

I channeled a lot of my anger and frustration during boot camp and the years that followed. I had to admit, it was satisfying to see Anna eye me when she thought I wasn't paying attention. Gone was the boy she'd left behind without a care in the world four and a half years ago. In his place was a man...a bigger, stronger, and better man.

I opened my email and scrolled through the usual video game newsletters and spam, deleting half of what was there. Then I paused. Near the bottom of my inbox was an email from her.

Anna.

The mouse's arrow hesitated over the message. Did I want to read this? Did I want to know what she had to say?

The answer was a resounding yes. I'd been waiting more than four years for the girl to talk to me. To talk to her. Without another moment's hesitation, I opened the message and poured over her words, re-reading it several times before finally sitting back in my seat.

She was sorry.

She was scared.

She hadn't wanted to feel.

My chest tightened. She'd been hurting so badly. I knew it back then. I did. Part of me went right back to that place, wishing I could have done more for her. But another part, the rational part, knew I'd done everything I could. She wasn't ready then.

But it sounded like she was ready now.

She wanted to send me something. I had no idea what it might be, but I was curious. I couldn't help it.

What would she think when she found out I was only a few hours north of her in Norfolk? I hoped she wouldn't want to visit. I wasn't ready for that. Responding to her email was difficult enough.

I thought email would be a safe, impersonal way to communicate, but I was wrong. Nothing about me and Anna was impersonal. It never had been, and it never would be.

***

After the gym that night, I sat down in front of the computer, ready to respond to Anna. I invited her message, I couldn't ignore it.

To: Anna Romano
From: Ryan Jacobs
Subject: RE: Hello

Dear Anna,
It's good to hear from you. You seem to be adjusting well to being at home so far. I'm happy to hear that. I know you were apprehensive, but I also knew you had nothing to worry about. Hate to say it, but I told you so. You don't have to apologize, but I appreciate your need to do so. I know you were hurting back then, that things weren't quite right. I had no idea the depths of what you were experiencing, couldn't quite wrap my head around it, you know? The way I processed that day was so much different than you, and it took me a while to realize that that was perfectly okay. So don't apologize. It's in the past. Just get well, okay? And I only did what was right in

taking you home, so you don't have to thank me. Anna, I'm proud of you for recognizing that it was time to make a change. I'm proud of you for taking the steps necessary to get better. You should be proud of yourself, too. Don't undermine your progress. Even going to one therapy appointment is a positive step. Remember that, and celebrate it.

The Navy is everything I dreamed of and more. I love my job, and I love being part of something so much bigger than myself. It's a family here. I room with a guy I've known since boot camp. We have the same rating (job), and we've gotten lucky and ended up in the same places so far, though I doubt that will always be the case. I've been a lot of places and seen a lot of things. It's been an experience. I re-upped. Another four years. I really can't imagine doing anything else with my life. It's been that good.

I've got duty early tomorrow, so I'm going to cut this off. It was nice hearing from you.
Ryan

I typed my address at the bottom, then re-read the message. It was perfectly innocuous. My greatest fear was giving her hope. Not hope for her future—I wanted her to have that—but hope for a future with me. It would be better for both of us if we didn't return to that place. There was too much going on in my life for me to add Anna to it. It wouldn't be fair to her.

Friends.

That was all we could be.

Right.

When had Anna and I ever been able to just be friends? We practically started dating the moment we met. Then, we broke up and never spoke to one another again.

Until now...

~ 11 ~

Anna

Virginia. He was in Virginia. *So close.* My body tingled. I didn't want a relationship, but I wanted his friendship. Maybe, one day, I would be able to visit him. Or he could come back here. Either would be nice.

I picked up the photo envelope I had tucked away in one of my desk drawers. It was just the right size for the treehouse sketch, and the rigidness of the cardboard would keep the paper from bending. After carefully printing Ryan's name and address on the envelope, I slid the sketch inside and sealed it.

I'd ask Mom to stop by the post office after the soup kitchen tomorrow. It would be my third time going. Serving the community made me feel like I was doing something, and it felt good to help people. It grounded me.

Settling the envelope on the corner of my desk, I clicked to reply to Ryan's email.

To: Ryan Jacobs
From: Anna Romano
Subject: Virginia?

Dear Ryan,
I'm going to send your package tomorrow. I didn't realize you were so close. I knew you were just visiting Seattle, but for some reason, I thought you lived on the west

coast. Do you get home to see your parents often? I guess they still live here. I didn't ask, but I assumed you stayed at their house while you were here.

I've been volunteering with my mom. I don't think I mentioned that in my last message. I might have...I rambled a lot in that message, so I don't know. Sorry about that. Mom volunteers at the soup kitchen over off Central. It's rewarding. It feels so weird to say that I get any kind of value from working with people less fortunate. It feels wrong, like I shouldn't value that time because it's probably the worst time of their lives. They probably want to forget it, but I never will. When I was in Seattle, I lived off ramen noodles. I was one night of bad tips away from having to eat at a soup kitchen myself. I probably wouldn't have gone though. I think I would have been too scared, too ashamed. Is it crazy that I probably would have gone hungry before asking for help? I'm not sure why I just told you all that. I promised myself that I wouldn't erase anything I wrote though. That if I say it, it's because I have to get it out, you know?

I'm glad you're enjoying the Navy. Thank you for your service. I didn't say that to you when we were together, and I should have. It's because of people like you, that people like me can make stupid mistakes and then have the opportunity to correct them. So four more years, huh? Have you been overseas at all? Seems silly to ask that since you're in the Navy, and, well...boats. I guess I'm wondering if you've been in a war zone? Are you ever scared? What is your job? Will you tell me about it?

I'm not sure if I should talk about my sessions with Dr. Matson or not, but I'm going to tell you about them. A little at least. She had me think of activities I used to do before...and I did (reading, sketching, hiking), and now she's having me try to do them again. I really like her. I think I liked her back when I was in Three Lakes, too, but I was so scared and angry and numb that I didn't let myself feel it. I'm glad she agreed to see me again. Anyway, I've been sketching and reading. Ronnie lent me her e-reader. She has a lot of romance novels. I just started one about a fighter. It's so different from the young adult stuff I used to read, but I like it. I haven't hiked yet, it's a little cold for that. Which is kind of ironic since I lived in Seattle for so long, and the North Carolina cold is nothing like Seattle cold, but it's funny...ever since I got warm, I haven't wanted to be cold.

Thanks for writing me back, Ryan. My family has been great, and I enjoy being back home with them, but it's nice having a friend.

Take care,
Anna

As I clicked send, there was a knock on my bedroom door. I quickly closed the web browser and slammed the screen down on my laptop, as if I'd been doing something wrong. I wasn't ready for my family to know I was talking with Ryan yet. I didn't want them to see it as something more than it was, a friendship.

I hurried to the door and opened it, seeing my dad on the other side. "Hey, Dad. What's up?"

"Hi, sweetheart. What are you up to?" He leaned in and gave me a kiss on the cheek.

"I was just getting ready to read a book Ronnie loaned me."

"Ah," he said, shaking his head. He must have known the kinds of books Ronnie read. "She's asking for your downstairs."

"Okay, I'll be right down."

He nodded, then turned away.

I closed the door and leaned my back against it. That was close. It wasn't a big deal to me that Ryan and I were talking again. I just didn't want my family to get the wrong idea. That was it. *Purely platonic,* I told myself.

Sure, I still had feelings for Ryan. I'd probably always love him. But it wasn't the same kind of feelings as before. Maybe someday I'd be ready to fall in love...but maybe never again with Ryan. The way I'd brushed him off was harsh. Even though he told me not to apologize, he probably wouldn't ever want a relationship with me again.

How could he ever forgive me for breaking his heart?

There was no use in thinking about it, though. We were friends, and that was that.

***

"He is the ultimate alpha male. The alpha all other alphas should be based off of. Don't you think?"

Ronnie was currently gushing about the fighter in the book I was supposed to be reading. As one of her favorites, she'd read it several times. She remembered parts of the plot and descriptions I couldn't remember, and I was currently reading it.

"Uh...yeah. He's really great."

She blew out a frustrated breath. "You're not even into it, Anna."

I glanced at her, raising my eyebrows. She was stretched out on her bed, and I was on the chaise by the window in her first floor bedroom. Her Kindle was propped up on my chest, and she was reading off the app on her iPad.

"I'm into it, Ronnie. That's why I'm reading it and not talking. Are you bored with your book?"

"Psh. I'm lost in the world of a sexy, alpha billionaire. I'm totally into it. I just like to talk books! You're killing me." She dropped her iPad onto her lap and closed her eyes, resting one arm across her face. She was impossible. Impossible and dramatic.

Setting the Kindle down, I resigned myself to talk alpha billionaires. "Okay, what do you want to talk about?"

"Never mind," she said, lifting her iPad and continuing to read.

Picking up the Kindle again, I proceeded with the story, hiding my smile behind the e-reader.

"You're going to have to get your own Kindle. This thing gets heavy after a while,"

Ronnie whined after a moment, tipping her iPad back and forth for emphasis.

"I'll see what I can do."

"See that you do," she retorted sassily, and I grinned.

Sisters.

I loved it.

~ 12 ~

Anna

"What's been going on since our last session?" Dr. Matson asked me once we were both settled in her small office. I chose to sit in one of the arm chairs this time, leaving the couch for Dr. Matson, just to change things up a little bit.

"I've sketched a little...and I'm reading a book," I added as an afterthought.

"That's great," she said, a genuine smile taking over her face. "Anything else?"

Did I tell her the truth? She was bound by confidentiality, so she couldn't tell my parents. Not that I was doing anything wrong.

"I've been emailing with Ryan. Nothing major, just sort of catching up. I apologized to him and also thanked him for helping me get back home."

She nodded, her brows drawn. "How has corresponding with Ryan made you feel?"

I chuckled internally at her very therapist-like question. "Good. Relieved. I don't know."

"Those are powerful feelings for you to have, Anna. You shouldn't underestimate them. In our first session, you described your feelings as guilty, numb and scared. Now you're using positive descriptors. That's a good thing."

"I guess."

"What else is there? I feel like you might be leaving something out."

She was so darn perceptive. "I haven't told my family that Ryan and I are talking."

"Why's that?"

"I don't want them to think something is going on that isn't."

"What *is* going on?"

"Nothing. We're just friends. It's nice to have a friend again, someone outside of my family to talk to."

"Have you been having any conflicts at home?"

"No," I stiffened and spit the next words out. "Why would you think that?"

"I don't think that. I was only asking because you said it was nice having someone outside of your family to talk to."

I relaxed back in my seat, which was difficult to do because the back of the armchair was as hard as a board. I was so taking back the couch next session.

"There's nothing wrong at home. They've been great. It's just...they treat me with kid gloves, you know? I understand why, I guess. They're probably afraid I'll break again...or run. So it's nice to talk to Ryan because I don't feel like he's analyzing everything I do or say."

"Let's get back to you not telling your family that you're talking to him. You said you don't want them to think something is going on."

"They might think we're going to get back together or something. We're not."

"You said you weren't ready for that," she reminded me of my words from the last session.

"I'm not. I don't want a relationship. I just

81

want a friend, but all Ryan and I have ever been is more than friends. I'm not sure they'd believe me that nothing was going on. They have no reason to trust me."

"They trust Ryan," she said. It wasn't a question.

"Yeah, they do," I agreed.

"You're afraid they won't believe your words."

"That and my feelings," I say quietly, studying the brown shag carpet under the small coffee table in the center of the space.

"Your feelings?"

"Yeah, like they might think I don't know what I'm feeling. They might think, 'Poor Anna, she doesn't even realize she's crushing on Ryan.'"

"You feel like their lack of trust spreads beyond just your words and actions to your emotions as well?"

"Can't really blame them if they feel that way, right?" I asked, looking up at her briefly. "I haven't given them a whole lot of reason to trust me, physically or emotionally."

"Have you given them any reason not to trust you since you've been home?"

"No. I don't think so. But how *could* they trust me? They remember the daughter and sister who stopped speaking, physically harmed herself, then took off for years. Why should they trust me?"

"I can't answer that for you, Anna. It sounds to me like you have a bit of resentment towards yourself for your actions. Have you considered forgiving yourself?"

No, I hadn't considered that. I shook my head.

"Anna, I think you might be painting yourself in a negative light because you're still upset with yourself. I think the feelings you're imagining your family having towards you are a reflection of how you feel about yourself. Does that make sense?"

Oddly, yes. It made perfect sense. But was it true?

I *was* disgusted with myself for the way I'd hurt my family...the way I hurt Ryan. Was I really projecting that onto other people the way Dr. Matson suggested? Maybe I was.

"It makes sense. I think...you might be right," I admitted.

"I want you to think about that between now and our next session. Maybe even make a list of the things you like about yourself. Good qualities you have. What are your assets?" I nodded my acceptance of the assignment. "Maybe consider keeping a journal," she suggested. "It might be neat to look back on so you can see your progress."

"Okay, I might do that." I liked journaling. I had a couple diaries as a kid. I never stuck with them, but they were fun while they lasted.

"Great," she said, slapping her hands on her legs. "So let's talk about your activities. What have you been reading and drawing?"

We spent the rest of the session talking about the images I'd drawn and the book Ronnie had lent me. I was a little embarrassed to share that last one, but she quickly diffused that when she turned around and made a few contemporary romance suggestions of her own. I never would have guessed she was a romance reader...it went to show you couldn't judge a book by its cover.

I left the session feeling even lighter.

The lightness didn't last long, though. As soon as I got home and checked my email, my heart dropped into my stomach. He was deploying.

Ryan was leaving.

~ 13 ~

Ryan

To: Anna Romano
From: Ryan Jacobs
Subject: RE: Virginia?

Dear Anna,
Yeah, I'm in Virginia. I'll be heading somewhere else after my deployment though, so I won't be here too much longer. Hopefully it's stateside, but I don't really get much of a choice in the matter.

Those books sound interesting. I don't read much unless it has to do with training or procedures. I had enough of that in high school, being forced to read whatever novel the English teachers deemed appropriate for our grade level. I always bought the Cliff's Notes, or looked up the plots online. And that's great that you've been sketching again. You always loved it, and you were so talented. It's cool you like Dr. Matson, that's gotta be helpful for you, right? Having someone you like to talk to. I hope everything works out for you, I really do.

My job with the Navy, they're called ratings, is air traffic control. I work behind the control panels inside the ship. It's stressful, but I enjoy it. I appreciate the challenge and the fact that I'm protecting our country. The ships I'm assigned to are aircraft carriers, those are the huge ones with the flat tops, like the Yorktown in Charleston. Remember when we visited there with your family one weekend? You sat on one of the cannons and I took your picture. Anyway, they're like floating cities, with post offices, general stores, medics, and financial and administrative offices. I have deployed before, twice. Once was just a six month cruise, it was more training than anything else. The other was a year over in the Middle East. Most of the activity over there is on land, so we weren't exactly in a war zone on the ship, not like you've probably seen on TV, but we were close enough to be in danger. I'm so busy on the ship, there really isn't time to get scared, though. It's usually the time before we deploy and while we're cruising when the nerves set in, but they train us on how to deal with that so it doesn't interfere with our work. We really can't make mistakes, so our mental well-being is always paramount.

I'm going to run (literally, I'm heading to the gym), but I'll talk to you soon.
Ryan

As I clicked send on the email, Rogers walked in with the mail, tossing a big envelope at me.

"What's this?" I asked.

"I don't fucking know," Rogers grumbled.

"It was a rhetorical question," I said back. He always got bitchy when we were getting ready to deploy. I didn't blame him, we all handled things differently. I knew that better than anyone.

Looking at the return address, I saw it was from Anna. I wasn't sure what I'd been expecting, but it wasn't an envelope. She said package, so my immediate thought was a box. I tore open the flap, pulled the sheet of paper from the inside and froze.

The treehouse.

She drew it, and it looked identical to the real thing. It was almost like I was staring at a black and white photo. She must have done it from memory, too, since the actual treehouse collapsed in a hurricane a few summers back. My reaction had been bittersweet when my parents told me of the loss. On the one hand, I was sorry to see the structure that held so many of mine and Anna's memories—intimate memories—go, but on the other hand it was like a form of closure. Like life was telling me it was time to move on.

Now this...

I navigated back to my inbox, ready to compose a new message to Anna, telling her I received the drawing, but there was already a new message from her. That was quick.

To: Ryan ,Jacobs
From: Anna Romano
Subject: RE: RE: Virginia?

Ryan,
When do you leave? How long will you be gone? Where are you going? Can you tell me?
Anna

I ran my hands through my hair, then rubbed them down my face. She was panicking. Part of me—a part deep down inside that had been buried a long time ago—wanted to pick up the phone and call her. That part of me wanted to reassure her that everything would be okay, that she didn't need to worry. The other part of me knew that calling her would be taking this...*thing*...that was between us too far.

Friends. We were just friends.

Didn't friends reassure each other, though?

There was a fine line for me and Anna. It had been years since we'd been in a relationship, but there was still that sizzle between us. I couldn't allow myself to do anything that would tip us over the edge.

Things were still too raw. We needed to build this friendship thing, and the best way to do that was to keep a distance. Email was one of the most impersonal forms of communication, so it would have to stay that way.

To: Anna Romano
From: Ryan Jacobs
Subject: RE: RE: RE: Virginia?

Anna,
I'll be gone on my deployment for eight months. We'll be at sea for most of that time, but we will stop at a few ports. I leave in a few weeks, and there's a lot I have to do in that time to prepare since I'll be going to a new base after I return. It's nothing for you to worry about. It's all routine stuff and

we can still email while I'm gone. There may be blackout periods where coms are down, but for the most part things stay up and running. Just focus on you. Keep sketching, reading, and when the weather is right, hike. They carved a new trail over at Forest Park. It's mostly used by mountain bikers, but it's good for hiking, too. You should check it out. There's also the paved bicycle paths down by Harmon's Creek, you can take Ronnie with you there. I'm sure she'd like to spend some time outside with you. I have to get going, but please don't worry about me, Anna. Everything will be okay.

Ryan

PS I got your sketch. It's amazing. I knew you still had it in you.

~ **14** ~

Anna

Two Months Later

After weeks of non-stop studying, I was finally finished with the GED exam.

Dropping out of high school was something I'd been ashamed of, something that was holding me back. Not anymore. I was all about new beginnings. And today was exactly that—a new beginning. I could finally apply to art school.

I stepped out the front doors of Lakeside High School for the very last time and paused, taking a deep breath of the cool, crisp winter air.

As Ryan and I once dreamed about years ago, today was the first day of the rest of my life.

Ryan.

He deployed a few weeks ago. I didn't get to see him again before he left. It was hard knowing he was even further away now, but he'd been right—we were still emailing, and things still felt the same because of that. Through our messages, we caught each other up on what we'd been doing with our days. Well, he shared what he was able to, which was mostly routine stuff around the ship. He couldn't really talk about his job, and I understood that. I told him about volunteering with Mom and the people I'd met. He encouraged me to get through my studying, and I told him what I'd been sketching. I did brave the cold and hit the new hiking trail he'd mentioned. When I reached the top, I sat and sketched the view. I mailed that picture to him last week. I knew it would take a while for it to reach him at sea, but I wanted him to see it—the real thing, not a picture of it.

He'd become such a big part of my life again, in a new way. I liked being friends with Ryan. We'd skipped that part when we first met eight years ago. In a way, it was another new beginning.

"What the heck are you doing?" Ronnie called, snapping my attention to the parking lot. She sat in her chair inside the handi-capable van—as she called it—with my dad behind the wheel. She and I were going to hit the bike trail.

"I'm coming," I hollered back, stepping off the curb and walking across the paved lot. I hopped in the van, sitting in the bucket seat beside her.

"How'd you do?"

"I aced it," I said confidently. "Piece of cake."

"Ooh, cake. Dad, can we get some cake on the way home?" Ronnie asked, and I laughed.

"Sure, honey." We were so spoiled—true daddy's girls—even in our twenties. He never could said no to either one of us, especially these days.

Dad dropped us off at the beginning of the trail, and I opened the back of the van to get my bike. Ronnie was bundled up in her power chair with a blanket—lucky—and I was set to go on my new bike.

"I'll be back in an hour. Just call me if you

need me to pick you up earlier."

"Bye, Dad!" Ronnie called, already scooting down the path.

"Watch out for her," Dad said as Ronnie moved out of earshot.

"Will do," I assured him.

"Proud of you, kiddo," he said, then got in the van and pulled away.

A small smile graced my face as I fastened my helmet and then pedaled hard to catch up with my sister.

"Jeez, you're slow," Ronnie said when I finally caught up.

"Hey, you're running off a motor. I'm running off pedal power," I huffed. Man, I was out of shape.

"Quit whining. At least your legs work."

My jaw dropped. "I didn't mean-"

Ronnie laughed. "Gotcha. You're so easy."

"Brat," I muttered under my breath.

"I heard that," she sang.

"You were meant to."

"Have you talked to Ryan lately?" she asked a few minutes later.

A few days before Ryan left, Ronnie caught me in a down moment. I was upset about the deployment, and I didn't want her to worry that I was regressing, so I told her the truth. I told her that Ryan and I had been talking through email and that I was sad he was deploying. She said all the right sisterly things, and since then I've updated her every now and then.

"I haven't heard from him in a few days, but he warned me that there was a blackout period coming up, so that's probably why."

"What's that?"

"Just a period of time when communications are down. They can't use the phone or internet."

"Oh. Well, that kind of sucks."

"I agree, but it's routine." We paused near a bench by the creek, and I lowered the kickstand on my bike. "I want to sit for a minute."

"Wimp."

I rolled my eyes and sat on the bench, taking off my helmet and trying to smooth my helmet hair. The chill on the surface bit right through my jeans, and I shivered.

"Do you miss him?"

"It's kind of hard to miss him when we haven't really spent time together," I told her. "But I guess I miss the idea of him. From before, you know?"

"Is it still just 'friendship' between the two of you?" she asked using air quotes around the word friendship.

"Yep," I answered, rolling my eyes and popping my lips on the P.

"Do you want more?"

"Not yet."

"But someday?"

I looked at the crystal clear water flowing in the creek, considering whether or not I wanted to be honest with my sister...with myself.

"I'm still not ready, but I'd be lying if I said I don't wonder if things could be different for us in the future. We haven't talked about it...at all. Everything we've talked about has been neutral. We avoid the heavy topics and we don't talk about feelings or anything like that, unless I tell him about one of my sessions."

"Do you guys ever talk about your relationship before?"

"No. We're always very careful to skirt around the edges of the past. We may mention a memory, but we never say that we were making out right before it happened or anything like that." Though I was always thinking about those moments. I wondered if he was, too.

"You guys are so weird. He loves you. You love him. You're exactly right, you're both just skirting around it all."

"I'm not ready for a relationship, Ronnie. I need to get myself well, first."

"You've been seeing Dr. Matson twice a week for over two months--"

"There's no set time--" I interrupted her, but she continued.

"I see an improvement in you, Anna. Mom and Dad do, too. You've made a lot of positive changes. I'm not saying you need to jump into a relationship. But maybe you should step a toe over the line a bit. Now is the perfect time to explore your feelings with Ryan since you're separated and can't physically act on anything."

"What do you mean?" I looked towards her, cautiously intrigued.

"Maybe bring up some of the hotter moments. See if he shuts them down, or if he acknowledges them."

"I don't know," I said, looking back to the creek. The rocks below the clear water were dark green from the algae. I remembered playing in the creek as a kid with Ronnie. The smooth rocks always felt slimy under my feet.

"Well, you're never *gonna* know unless you try."

"Maybe. I'll think about it."

"All you ever do is think. You need to act!"

"You need to stop reading so many romance novels," I laughed as she scowled at me, muttering something about how it was a way of life. She was too much.

"Come on, let's go."

By the time I'd put my helmet back on and mounted my bike, she was already a good distance ahead of me. I pedaled hard and caught up. "Cheater," I teased.

"You're just jealous," she teased back.

~ **15** ~

Ryan

The blackout was lifted last night, so I was finally able to get on the computer. We were only without coms for about a week, but I missed the interaction with the outside world. I was back in the communications room after my shift to have a video call with Kelsey, and while I waited, I checked my email. Anna had replied to my last message, and to say I was a little surprised by her response was an understatement.

To: Ryan Jacobs
From: Anna Romano
Subject: Hi

Dear Ryan,
It was good to hear from you again. I missed talking to you. I'd gotten pretty used to it. It reminded me of that time you went on that Alaskan cruise with your parents your junior year. I wished your parents would have just let you stay with us like my parents had offered, but our reunion was worth it, don't you think?

She went on to say more, but I couldn't really focus on that. All I could think about was the memory she'd shared and how provocative it was. We'd had sex for the first time after I returned from that trip.

Surely she wasn't...

I re-read the beginning of the message. She definitely was.

She and I hadn't crossed that kind of line in our communication. Not once. It was safer that way. For her and for me. She needed to get well and I...I needed to not get my heart involved. Not again. She was still too fragile, too capable of breaking it.

I stared at her message for a while, not knowing how to reply. Did I mention the metaphorical elephant she so kindly placed in the room or did I ignore it? I didn't want her to think that our time together had meant nothing to me. Would ignoring her words imply that? I didn't want to encourage that kind of conversation either.

Rock, meet hard place. Fuck.

I tapped my finger on the edge of the desk, thinking about how I'd reply. A ping from the computer's speaker pulled me out of my head, and I saw that Kelsey had signed on to Skype. I clicked her circle to call her, eager to see my girl.

"Hey," Kelsey's pretty face filled the screen. She was always so cheerful, so positive, despite the challenges life threw at her. "Charlotte's been asking for her daddy all day."

Unable to hold back my cheesy grin, I tried to rein in my emotions before our daughter came on. Nothing could bring a grown man to his knees quite like his little girl. "Is that right? Well, I've been waiting to see her all day, so we're even."

Kelsey laughed and leaned down to pick up Charlotte, then my baby girl's beautiful face was looking back at me.

"Daddy!" she squealed, drawing the attention of some of the other guys in the room. I turned the speakers down a little bit. She had the tendency to shout into the computer when we chatted.

"Hey, princess. How are you?"

"Good. I had ice cweam today."

"Did you? What kind?"

"Chocowate wif spwinkles."

I gave her a watery smile. I loved the way she lisped out certain words. She was adorable, perfect in every way, and that wasn't just the biased opinion of her father. It was fact.

"That's my favorite."

"It's my faborite, too, Daddy."

"How is school?" Not yet three years old, she didn't go to an actual school; she went to daycare while Kelsey worked, and we called it school.

"It fun. I wove it."

"Good, princess. That's really good. You like your new house?"

She nodded, looking towards something off the screen. As usual, our conversations lasted about two minutes before something else took her toddler attention.

"Why don't you go play sweetie, we'll talk again soon."

"Okay, Daddy. I wove you."

"I love you, too, princess." She scampered off and Kelsey took the screen again. "How did the move go?" They'd just relocated to San Diego, where my next assignment was.

"It went really well." She was always smiling, always the optimist, even when she

98

told a scared, barely twenty year-old kid he was going to be a dad. "The apartment is great, too. Are you sure you can afford this?"

"Yes. They give military discounts, and I'm saving by rooming with Rogers."

"If you're sure. I can pitch in more," she tried to argue.

Shaking my head, I shut her down immediately. "You already pitch in enough. You pretty much raise Charlotte on your own ninety percent of the time. It's the least I can do." And it was true. Kelsey was an amazing mother. We might not have worked out on an intimate level, but we co-parented Charlotte like we'd been training our whole lives for it.

I'd never forget the day she showed up at the bar we'd met at three months before. It was a dive, known for being a military hang out due to its proximity to the base in Everett. Kelsey and I met there one night, got drunk, and one thing led to another. She was the first—the only—person I'd slept with since Anna. Admittedly, I'd used her to try to fill the void Anna had left behind, but it didn't work. She, too, was just looking for a release. We'd said goodbye the next day and parted amicably. I never thought I'd see her again. Color me surprised when she showed up at that same bar three months later, telling me she was pregnant.

I never questioned her, I didn't have a reason to. She was a successful woman, five years older than me and had no reason to try to trap a young, broke enlistee. The pregnancy was as much an inconvenience for her as it was to me, but we owned it. We tried a relationship—went out on one date—and it just wasn't happening. The drunken chemistry we'd shared was non-existent sober. Six months later, Charlotte Elise was born, and our worlds were never the same.

Fortunately, she worked from home designing websites, so she could live anywhere. When I left Washington State for Virginia, she and Charlotte were able to come with me. Now, I moved them to California. It couldn't have been easy on her, but she didn't have any close family, so she always insisted it was fine.

"Thanks for doing this, Kels."

"No problem. Charlotte should be near her dad. I'm not saying I'll be able to follow you every time you move. Once Charlotte is in school, it'll be more difficult."

"And you might meet someone someday."

"Yeah," she laughed. "There's just a line of guys out there looking for a woman with a toddler."

"You never know," I told her.

"Yeah, well, when the time comes, you'll be the first to know."

I nodded, still smiling at the screen. "I know."

"Have you heard from Anna?" Kelsey asked, a softer look on her face.

Over the years, Kelsey had become a good friend, maybe even a best friend. I told her all about Anna, our reunion, and the emails. It helped to have a female perspective sometimes, especially since I couldn't talk about this kind of thing with Rogers.

"Yeah, I was just reading an email from her before I called you."

"And?"

Maybe Kelsey could give me advice on how to reply to Anna's message. The innuendo seemed so clear, but still I was at a loss. I decided to tell Kelsey what Anna said, and we spent the rest of the time before Charlotte's bath time talking about my feelings and what I should say to her.

I should have probably hung up my man card right then and there.

~ 16 ~

Anna

Ryan took two days to respond to my email. I spent those days cursing myself for mentioning the Alaskan cruise and what happened after. I cursed Ronnie, too, for suggesting it. I just knew I'd scared him away.

But then he wrote back...and what he said blew me away.

It was the best night of my life.

I couldn't remember what the rest of his message said. I re-read those eight words over and over again. I'd thrown the innuendo out there, he caught it, and threw it back. What happened next?

Where did I go from there?

To: Ryan Jacobs
From: Anna Romano
Subject: Package

Dear Ryan,
Have you received the package I sent you yet? It's another sketch I thought you might like. I'm just wondering how long it takes for things to get from here to there. Things here have been good. I'm just waiting on the results of my GED exam so I can apply to art school. Keep your fingers crossed for

me, okay?

Anna

Avoidance.

That was how I was going to handle it. Real mature, Anna. Real mature.

I quickly added a PS.

PS All my memories with you took place on the best days of my life.

Before I had the chance to second guess myself, I hit send.

***

I spent the afternoon reviewing the application process for Braddock Art Institute. I'd have to look into my portfolio to see if I had pieces that would match their submission requirements, otherwise I'd have to create some new things.

Technically, I couldn't apply until October, which was a long ways away—and even then it would be for admission the following fall—but my old high school art teacher, Mrs. Martin, had some connections in the school's art department, and was going to explain my situation to see if she could pull some strings. I hated using my victim status to get something, but I wanted this so badly. If I could end up in art school an entire year early, I would do volunteer work for the rest of my life.

Which reminded me...next stop on the internet, soup kitchens near Braddock. I fully intended to continue my volunteer work, even if I wasn't able to do it as frequently due to my class schedule.

My computer pinged, and I saw it was the messenger app linked to my email provider. I never used it before, so I wasn't quite sure how it worked, but I saw a little green icon blinking, so I clicked it.

A message from Ryan popped up.

Ryan Jacobs: PS? Really?

What was he talking about? PS?

Wracking my memory, I finally remembered and my hands flew up to my mouth as my eyes widened. I couldn't believe he was confronting me about it!

Anna Romano: I was really concerned about the package.
Ryan Jacobs: Uh huh.
Anna Romano: Have you gotten it yet?
Ryan Jacobs: No, it can take weeks. I told you that.

He did tell me that, and it had only been a little more than seven days since I'd sent it.

Anna Romano: Okay.
Ryan Jacobs: Can we talk about what we're not talking about?
Anna Romano: I guess so.

The conversation was so weird, but it shouldn't be. I was talking to Ryan! I'd always been able to talk to him about anything. It was different now, though. I felt like a teenage girl with a crush, something we hadn't had in the beginning since we jumped right into dating.

A friendship...then a crush...that was the natural path things like this took, right?

The computer pinged again.

Ryan Jacobs: This shouldn't be weird.
Anna Romano: That's what I was just thinking!
Ryan Jacobs: Great minds...
Anna Romano: Yeah.
Ryan Jacobs: What are you thinking about?
Anna Romano: What do you mean?
Ryan Jacobs: About us. You and me. What are you thinking about us? What do you want us to be?
Anna Romano: I don't know, Ryan. I'm a little confused.
Ryan Jacobs: Me too.

At least I wasn't the only one.

It was all so surreal. I hadn't expected him to want to talk about it. I thought it would be a little harmless enquiring. Ryan always was direct, though.

I just had to be honest, right?

Anna Romano: I know I care a lot about you, and I miss you. I miss how easy things used to be.
Ryan Jacobs: Why'd you mention the cruise?
Anna Romano: I'm so embarrassed, Ryan. That's Ronnie's fault.
Ryan Jacobs: Explain?
Anna Romano: This is so embarrassing.
Anna Romano: Okay, so we were talking the other day and she asked about you.

She knows there's nothing going on between us, I told her I wasn't looking for a relationship, that I wanted to focus on getting better. She asked if I still had feelings for you.
Ryan Jacobs: And?

My face flushed with embarrassment. Yeah, Ronnie had suggested I mention something from when we were dating, but I was the one who dove right in and brought up the first time we'd had sex...when I lost my virginity to him. Ohmygod. I couldn't have referenced our first kiss? Or a time we'd snuggled? Nope. Ryan wasn't the only one who was direct...

Anna Romano: I told her I thought I might, but I didn't know how you felt. That we usually skirted around the subject of our dating history in our emails. So she suggested I bring it up...to see how you responded.
Ryan Jacobs: So that moment is what you chose to bring up?

Gah!!

Anna Romano: I know!! It's just that the whole radio silence thing really did remind me of the time you went on that cruise, so it fit the moment.
Ryan Jacobs: I see.
Anna Romano: Did I just ruin this?

Minutes ticked by as I awaited his response, chewing my fingernail. Did I scare him off? The icon was still lit next to his name, so he hadn't signed off.

Ugh.

Ryan Jacobs: You didn't ruin anything, Anna. Just caught me by surprise is all. I know we don't talk about the past, not that much anyway, but I don't want you to think, not for one minute, that I've forgotten about it. About us. I think about you and all the times we had all the time. Some of those memories got me through some difficult times. I do still care about you, a lot. I don't think those feelings will ever change. I haven't let myself think of you as more than a friend since we started talking again because I know you're not ready. You still have a lot of emotions to work through. I'm not sure I'm ready for that either, at least not while I'm away and can't act on anything. But Anna, I do think about being with you again sometimes. You're one of the most special people in my life, and maybe one day, we can see what happens.

Mush. I was a puddle of mush. His words...

Anna Romano: I understand.
Ryan Jacobs: We good?
Anna Romano: No. We're great.

~ **17** ~

To: Ryan Jacobs
From: Anna Romano
Subject: Pop Culture

Dear Ryan,
I feel like I've been living under a rock the last four years. Not only are Ronnie's books totally different than anything I'd read before, but there are movies and TV shows and music I know absolutely nothing about.

Ronnie lent me her iPod and she has all this new music on it, well, new to me. Lorde, Sam Smith, Hozier, and Meghan Trainor are just a few. I'm overwhelmed! And all these superhero TV series and movies? I wish I could go back in time and DVR them all. Netflix and Hulu will have to do. I was bummed to see The Vampire Diaries *and* Grimm *are in their final seasons, but at least I still have* Supernatural. *I can't believe all the ghost hunting shows that are on these days, though! I don't know which to watch, so I record them all.*

I'm so overwhelmed by all this new entertainment. Please, give me some direction!

Totally lost,

Anna

To: Anna Romano
From: Ryan Jacobs
Subject: RE: Pop Culture

Anna,
First of all, you're listening to the wrong music. That's the problem. Don't be taking musical advice from Ronnie. She's probably one square away from boy band bingo. Rock music is where it's at. Download the Pandora app on your cell phone and check out Adelitas Way, Theory of a Deadman, and Seether. It'll play some of their songs, and songs like them. I guarantee you'll find some songs you like. Then we'll talk music. I haven't watched much TV in a while, so I can't really help you out there. But you've got to catch up on the Batman *and* Avengers *movies. That's an order!*
Ryan

To: Ryan Jacobs
From: Anna Romano
Subject: No thank you!

Dear Ryan,
Sorry, I'm not into that screamy stuff you listen to, so I'll pass on your musical selections and stick to what I know...Katy Perry and Taylor Swift. And really? You don't watch TV anymore? Even Supernatural? *That kind of breaks my heart a little bit, Ryan. That first day...in art*

109

class, you started talking to me because I was sketching the anti-possession tattoo that Sam and Dean have. After that, I always looked forward to our weekly ritual of cookie dough ice cream and Supernatural.

And you're ordering me around now? Don't worry, I'm already caught up on all the different Avengers' movies. I think I'll watch Guardians of the Galaxy *next. I was kind of hoping that maybe we could watch some together, too, when you get back. Even if we have to do it over Skype. It would be fun. It's been so long since we've watched a movie together.*

Talk to you soon,
Anna

To: Anna Romano
From: Ryan Jacobs
Subject: Listen to the music.

Anna,
Seriously, listen to the music. It's not all screaming stuff. I know you don't like that stuff, so I wouldn't do that to you. The bands I suggested have some lighter stuff. And, while you're at it, check out "Blank Space" by I Prevail. It's a cover of Taylor Swift. It's pretty good, but a little "screamy."

I'm glad you're catching up on your superheroes. I'm definitely down for some catching up when I get back to the States.

110

We'll figure it out. Guardians of the Galaxy *was awesome, good choice.*

It was hard watching Supernatural *without you. It was our thing, you know? Plus, I didn't have much free time to watch TV when I first enlisted. Then when I did watch it, it felt like something was missing. Maybe we can catch up on that sometime, too.*

Your musical genius,
Ryan

To: Ryan Jacobs
From: Anna Romano
Subject: Not so bad…

Dear Ryan,
*Well, I'm not going to admit I was wrong since there were still some screamy songs, but I liked the bands you suggested, and the others that came up on the station. Breaking Benjamin is cool, too. Of course, Ronnie is freaking out because something other than Top 20 is playing in the house. *rolling my eyes**

I get what you mean…about Supernatural, *I tried to watch some old episodes online and it wasn't the same for me either. Things are so different now than they were back then, you know? Times have changed so much that I'm not constantly reminded of our time together. Different songs play on the radio, different commercials on the TV…but every once in a while something*

111

reminds me of you, and I hold on to those moments as tightly as I can. It's not like I'm afraid I'm going to forget you, that will never happen, I just miss you a lot, I guess.

So the latest book Ronnie has loaned me is hilarious. It's about a girl, her dad, and her brother taking a cross country trip before her brother gets married and her brother's best friend joins them. I've laughed so hard in parts I actually snorted. It made me think of the first time I snorted in front of you. I thought I'd die of embarrassment!

Blushing,
Anna

To: Anna Romano
From: Ryan Jacobs
Subject: Porky Pig

Anna,
I'd forgotten all about that. We were watching Ron White, weren't we? That was hilarious. I called you Porky for weeks after that. It wasn't as funny as the time you farted though.

Holding my nose,
Ryan

To: Ryan Jacobs
From: Anna Romano
Subject: What?!

Ryan,
I don't even know what you're talking about. I don't fart.

Anna

To: Anna Romano
From: Ryan Jacobs
Subject: Yes, you do.

Dear Anna,
Babe, everyone farts. Nothing to be ashamed of. No one can hold it in when they eat that much bean dip, they'd explode. That'll teach you. Which reminds me, Cinco de Mayo is in a couple months! Do you have anything fun planned now that the warmer weather is settling in?

Still holding my nose,
Ryan

To: Ryan Jacobs
From: Anna Romano
Subject: Summer

Dear Ryan,
Yeah, Ronnie has a list of things she wants me to do with her. There are a bunch of local food festivals coming up, and some art ones, too. My parents are talking about celebrating the Fourth of July on the lake. It's been so long since I've done that, I'm looking forward to it. Last time I saw fireworks was with you, in more ways than

one. ;)

I should be getting my GED results soon. I hope I passed so I can start the college applications. I've been volunteering so much with Mom, I feel like my resume is quite padded in that department, but I kind of regret not getting a job since I've been home. I was just so focused on getting well that I didn't even think about it. Plus, I worked my butt off while I was gone, so I could use the break.

I'd better go. Ronnie has implemented mandatory book meetings on Mondays and Thursdays where I must discuss with her whatever book she's forced me to read.

Miss you,
Anna

PS The books aren't as much of a hardship as I make them out to be. I actually kind of like them, but giving Ronnie a hard time is too much fun.

To: Anna Romano
From: Ryan Jacobs
Subject: You'll pass.

Dear Anna,
Don't worry about the GED. You're the smartest person I know and you studied your ass off. You're going to ace that thing, no question about it. Have a little faith in yourself, I do.

114

So, you're just going to avoid the whole fart conversation, huh?

I'm glad you're liking the books. Have you read that one with the whips and chains they turned into a movie? Is that what you're reading, Anna? Sexy books? You dirty, dirty girl. You seriously have to tell me because I have all these wild thoughts running through my head, and in most of them, you're not wearing much. ;)

Your naughty dreamer,
Ryan

To: Ryan Jacobs
From: Anna Romano
Subject: You're such a guy!

Dear Ryan,
I'm so not telling you anything else about the books I'm reading. That topic of conversation is off the table.

Thanks for believing in me. You have no idea how much it means to hear you say that. I've made so many mistakes, it makes it hard to have faith in myself, but you give me that. I appreciate it.

Love,
Anna

Ryan Jacobs: Whatcha reading?

Anna Romano: Can it, Jacobs.

Ryan Jacobs: No can do.

Anna Romano: I'm not telling you anything.

Ryan Jacobs: I knew it!

Anna Romano: Knew what?

Ryan Jacobs: You are reading the sexy books.

Ryan Jacobs: I bet you did read the one with the whips.

Ryan Jacobs: Anna?

Ryan Jacobs: Hello?

Anna Romano: Goodbye, Ryan.

Ryan Jacobs: I'm like a dog with a bone, Anna, I'm not giving up.

Anna Romano: You're going to be greatly disappointed.

Ryan Jacobs: Doubt that.

Anna Romano: What makes you so confident?

Ryan Jacobs: Because I know I'm right.

Anna Romano: Hate to tell you this, but you're wrong. I haven't read that book.

Anna Romano: Yet...

*Ryan Jacobs: *groans**

Anna Romano: lol

~ **18** ~

Ryan

As the weeks progressed, it was more of the same. Anna and I would exchange emails, and I'd send her instant messages when we were online at the same time, which wasn't too often given the time difference and the odd hours I kept.

We talked about everything—day-to-day stuff, music, movies, her therapy sessions, and the past. Ever since that first night on messenger, we opened up to one another more, but I felt like shit because I still hadn't told her about Charlotte.

Kelsey asked me about it the last time we talked on Skype. She asked why I hadn't told Anna. I didn't have an answer for her.

Maybe I wasn't ready to pop the new bubble Anna and I were living in. Maybe I didn't want to hurt her or stress her out. While we'd been opening up to each other more and more, we hadn't discussed any of the relationships we'd had in the years we were apart. I had a feeling Anna wouldn't have much—if anything—to contribute to that conversation. Anna was making progress in her therapy, she'd done a complete one-eighty from the girl who tossed me out of her house and her life years ago.

I didn't want to set her back. Charlotte was an unexpected blessing in my life, and I wanted to share her with Anna when I knew

Anna could handle it.

So I kept Charlotte to myself, which meant I kept Kelsey to myself as well.

I hadn't told Anna about my orders yet either. It would be great if she ended up at art school in San Diego, because then we'd be in the same city. Telling Anna about San Diego would be much easier than telling her about Charlotte. I knew I had to share both pieces of information with her, and soon. I just hoped it wouldn't blow up in my face. A lie of omission was still a lie, wasn't that how the saying went? Shit.

Glancing at the sheet of paper before me, I realized that for the first time in a long time, I missed home. I had just received another sketch from Anna in the mail. The first one she sent me was gorgeous—the view from the top of the hiking trail. I loved seeing it through her eyes. The one in my hands was of the creek. She'd taken my advice, and she and Ronnie traveled the bike trail often. In her note, she said that they had some warmer days, so she sat on a bench and sketched while Ronnie read. The image came to life as I pictured the exact place she'd drawn it. There was only one bench on the trail, after all, and I'd sat in that same place more than once.

Clearing my head, I opened up a new email and began to type.

To: Anna Romano
From: Ryan Jacobs
Subject: Happy St. Patrick's Day

Dear Anna,
Do you and Ronnie have anything fun

planned for St. Patrick's Day? I remember the two of you used to go all out for holidays. Used to drive me crazy. In a good way, of course. Is the house all decorated? Ha, I guess you guys got it from your mom. I never really thought about that. It's cool though, it's cool you guys have those traditions. I wish my parents had been a little more traditional sometimes.

We've got some training exercises over the next few days, so I may not be able to get on my email. It's routine stuff we do periodically while we're out here, but they tend to be long days, and by the end I'm pretty wiped out. I'll message you if I can though.

I can't believe you want to go on a cruise! No offense, babe, but that's the last kind of vacation I want to go on. I love my job, no doubt about that, but I get my share of ships at work. And water. My ideal vacation these days would be a cabin in the mountains with snow or something. As far inland as I can get. But...if you wanted to go on a cruise, I'd take you. I'm beginning to think I'd do anything you asked me to do.

I love the new sketch. You are so talented. I knew you'd get your muse back if you just tried. I hope everything works out with school and Mrs. Martin is able to pull some strings. It's cool that she's still looking out for you after all these years. I always liked her. Of course, it was in her class where we met, so room 105 will always hold a special place in my heart.

You know...if you end up at Braddock, you'll be awfully close to me. I got my orders and I'll be heading to San Diego, too, after this tour. It would be nice to be able to see you anytime I want.

I've been thinking about taking some online classes for my bachelor's degree. If I ever want to go to OCS, officer's school, then I'll need a bachelor's degree. I don't know if I want to or not, but it's something I've been thinking about. Even if I don't choose to make a career out of the Navy, I'll need a degree to get a good job anyway, so it's not like it'll hurt anything. Too bad I don't know what I want to be when I grow up. I love the Navy, so it seems like the logical choice.

I'd better get going. I need to get some rest because the next few days are going to be brutal. Talk to you soon.

Ryan

~ **19** ~

Anna

Staring at the piles of paper on my desk, I realized that this was it. Everything I needed to complete the application process for Braddock Art Institute lay before me. I'd just gotten my GED test results and passed with flying colors. I even received a fancy certificate saying my scores were ranked with the top scores of the state. The entire state!

I couldn't wait to share the news with Ryan. After the happy bomb he dropped on me in his last email, I knew he'd be excited, too.

He was heading to San Diego; I was headed to San Diego (hopefully!).

Our teenage dreams were coming true. We always knew we'd spend four years apart, then start the rest of our lives together. It didn't happen exactly how we'd planned, but it was still happening. That had to count for something...right?

To: Ryan Jacobs
From: Anna Romano
Subject: Exciting News!

Dear Ryan,
First of all, I can't believe you were holding out on me. San Diego!? That's wonderful news.

I have some great news to share, too. I passed the GED! Not to brag, but I did really well on it, too. Mom, Dad, Ronnie, and I all went out for dinner and ice cream, kind of like how we used to when we got good report cards as kids. It was a lot of fun. Reminded me of some real happy times. The only thing missing was you, but you were there in my mind.

So I'm sitting here with a stack of papers on my desk, everything I need to get started on my Braddock application. I hope Mrs. Martin will be able to pull some strings and get me accepted sooner rather than later. I'm not holding my breath, but I am hopeful. Dr. Matson thinks this will be good for me. She tells me all the time how pleased she is with my progress and all the positive changes I've been making. My family, too. It's nice. It makes me feel awful for not allowing her to help me years ago.

Anyway, I better start sifting through this stuff. I'll talk to you soon.

Love,
Anna

Working diligently, it took me a few hours to complete the forms and type up my admissions essay. Speaking of my love of art was easy, but putting myself out there was not. I was used to my art being on display, not my words. I plowed through though, leaving my heart and soul on those pages...pouring all my passion into one thousand words. When I was finished, I re-read the piece and let out a contented sigh. That essay and my portfolio made me a shoe-in for art school.

I opened my email one more time before I shutdown my computer for the night. There was a response from Ryan.

To: Anna Romano
From: Ryan Jacobs
Subject: RE: Exciting News

Dear Anna,
Congratulations. I'm so proud of you. Even if you don't get into Braddock this fall, you'll get in for next year. I have faith in you. Your work is nothing short of amazing and they'd be fools not to see that. Fools or blind. If they don't want you, there are schools out there bigger and better than BAI, and they'd be lucky to have you.

You've got me craving ice cream, thank you very much. There's some on the ship, but it's not as good as the stuff we used to get from Scoops. That place was amazing. Is that where you went with your family? I remember all the times we went there, you always ended up with ice cream on the tip of your nose and I always ended up licking it off. You'd taste like butter pecan for hours after one of those trips. I miss that. I miss you. I don't know what's going on here, Anna, but I kind of like it. It feels like old times, like something I lost has been returned to me, and it feels good.

I'm glad things are going well in therapy. Don't beat yourself up about not completing therapy the first time. You weren't ready then, but you are now. That's the difference. That's why it's working. You're ready for change. Will Dr. Matson be referring you to someone in San Diego when you move? (Because you will be moving.) I know you're doing well, but moving and starting school can be stressful and you need to make sure you're taken care of. I don't want anything to happen to you. I have absolute faith in you and your progress, but I don't want something to set you back, you know? Please don't get upset with me for saying that. I care about you, that's all.

I watched a movie with some of the guys last night, Captain America. *Remember when we saw that in the theater? It was a double date with Ronnie and Derek the douche. Ronnie was so bored, but you loved it. When I get back to the States, I want to take you to the movies. We'll find whatever superhero flick is in the theaters and see it. If there isn't one, I guess we'll just have to rent one. Something new that neither of us have seen before. We can cuddle up on the couch with a blanket and some popcorn and chocolate...actually, screw the movie theater...we'll just find something to rent. ;)*

I gotta get going, but I wanted to respond quickly and tell you congrats. I'm proud of you. I knew you had it in you. You can do anything you want to do, A. Anything.

Ryan

My heart soared and my body heated at the memories he'd shared. What he left out of his email was that we made out like the teenagers we were when we watched *Captain America*. We had to stay for the next showing because we missed most of the first. Oh...and the part about the ice cream...I had to fan myself. Literally, fan myself. I hadn't been with anyone since Ryan. Not a date, not a kiss, nothing...and his reminiscence left me hot and bothered.

What was I going to do with him?

What was I doing with him?

I don't know what's going on here, Anna, but I kind of like it. It feels like old times, like something I lost has been returned, and it feels good.

Me, too, Ryan. Me, too.

~ **20** ~

Anna

"Welcome to Braddock Art Institute's Class of 2021."

I hadn't stopped smiling since I left the meeting with Mrs. Martin. The dean's words replayed themselves on repeat in my mind. We had a video conference with her colleague at the college, along with the Dean of the College of Fine Arts and the Dean of Admissions. They were all so impressed with my portfolio, which Mrs. Martin helped me get ready. I couldn't thank her enough. I hugged her with tears streaming down my face for a solid five minutes before I ran out of her studio and met my mom in the parking lot. Mom and I bounced and laughed and cried, celebrating the achievement.

I couldn't wait to tell Ryan, but I kind of wanted to surprise him, thinking it would be fun to meet him in San Diego when his flight came in. He would have no idea I was in San Diego, and I was certain I'd be able to get the details of his flight out of him. After months of emailing and messaging, we'd gotten closer, reminiscing about old times. I just knew he'd be excited to see me.

I logged onto my computer and opened my email, hoping for a message from him. I wanted to get my fill before Ronnie and I headed out to our favorite Mexican restaurant for Cinco de Mayo.

I frowned at the lack of email, but smiled when an instant message popped up.

Ryan Jacobs: Can you talk?
Anna Romano: Of course, what's up?

I loved being able to chat with him in real time on messenger. It lessened the distance between us...mentally at least.

Ryan Jacobs: Do you have Skype?
Anna Romano: Yeah, Ronnie made me get it so we could video chat.
Ryan Jacobs: You and Ronnie video chat from inside the same house?
Anna Romano: What's wrong with that?
Ryan Jacobs: You two are so lazy.
Anna Romano: Well, maybe I don't want to video chat with you.

Lie! Lie!! I totally wanted to video chat with him. I hadn't seen his face in months, and I was having withdrawals. Pictures just didn't cut it. They weren't the same.

Ryan Jacobs: Please, Anna. I need you.

That sobered me up. He needed me? Was something wrong?

Anna Romano: Is everything okay?
Ryan Jacobs: It will be. What's your user name?
Anna Romano: AnnaBanana1201. Don't laugh...Ronnie created it.

I opened Skype, logged in, and immediately

had an incoming video call. I clicked to accept, and then he was there. My smile spread so far across my face, my cheeks hurt.

"Hey," I said, giving a little wave.

"Hey," he said. His return smile was brief.

"What's going on?" I asked, concerned by the rigid set of his posture.

He looked over his shoulder, then moved closer to the computer screen.

Weird.

"We had some training exercises today. More routine stuff. It should have been routine." His brows creased and his voice was low, but frantic. "Something went wrong with one of the jets. The pilot had to eject. The plane...it crashed."

I gasped, raising my hand to my mouth. "Is he okay? Was anyone hurt?"

He exhaled a gust of breath and shook his head. "He was fine. He got out just in time. The jet hit the water a couple hundred yards away. It just...it scared the hell out of me, you know? We were lucky, so lucky."

"Do you know what went wrong?"

He scowled, his brows still knitted. "A dive team is working on retrieving the wreckage. The pilot reported some smoke in the cockpit before he ejected. I wasn't on the radio, so I don't know what all he said, that's just what was told to me. It was probably something mechanical."

"That must have been horrifying."

"It was. Everyone is safe, and I didn't do anything wrong, but it still shook me up real good." He lifted up a hand, and I watched it shake through the screen. I wanted to reach through and hug him. He curled his fingers into a fist, then spread them out...over and over again, as if expecting the digits to stop trembling.

"I'm so sorry, Ryan. Is there anything I can do?" He appeared so dejected, so exhausted.

"Just talk to me. I don't have long, but I love hearing your voice."

My heart melted into a puddle right there on the floor of my bedroom.

"I'm going for my road test tomorrow," I told him excitedly.

"It's about time," he said flatly.

"Hey! Be nice. I'm conquering one little thing at a time."

"I'm just teasing you. I'm proud of you, Anna. You're doing great."

"Thanks." Smiling shyly, I imagined how proud he would be if he knew I was going to Braddock. My smile spread into a grin as I thought about my plan to surprise him.

"What are you smiling about?"

"Nothing, I'm just happy to be talking to you."

"What else have you been up to?"

I told him what I did over the last few days. Nothing too exciting...more hiking, biking, and volunteering with mom. He smiled, nodded, and laughed in all the appropriate places.

Then he had to go.

"I'm sorry to cut this short, but I shouldn't even be in here. I just wanted to talk to you. I needed to see you."

"I'm here for you, Ryan. Anytime."

"Thanks, A."

"Bye," I waved, and he waved back before disconnecting the call.

I got up, walked over to my bed, and fell onto my back with a smile the size of Alaska on my face. I got to talk to him...I saw him! Rolling over, I tucked my face into my pillow and squealed.

Butterflies!

Butterflies had taken flight in my belly. That was the only way I could describe the feeling.

I knew...I just knew...I was falling in love with Ryan Jacobs all over again.

***

The next several days were spent reviewing the academic and course catalogs for Braddock. I was surprised when I realized I'd need to report for new student orientation in July...only two months away.

Time was flying by. Initially, the passage of time had excited me, it meant we were getting closer to the end of Ryan's deployment. But now it meant something different. It meant I'd be moving soon. Was I ready for that?

Anxiety streamed through my veins like a thick soup as I looked at the dates, the required courses, and the countless other things I'd need to address over the coming weeks.

It was real. This was happening. I was going to art school.

And I was terrified.

~ **21** ~

Anna

"I don't know if I can do this."

"It's perfectly normal to feel anxious and apprehensive. This is a big step." I met Dr. Matson's eyes across the room. Her encouraging smile was almost enough...almost. She sighed, realizing her reassurances weren't enough. They'd never be enough. "Anna, you're making great progress. What's holding you back?"

The unknown.

Being all alone on the other side of the country.

Missing my family.

"I can see the wheels turning," she mused, one corner of her mouth tipping up.

"I don't know," I lied.

"Anna," she urged, using that mom-tone she took with me when she knew I was holding something back.

I blew out a breath, pressing myself against the back of the loveseat in an effort to stop my body from trembling. "I'm scared. I'm scared of everything. Moving, starting school, being away from my family...so far away. I'm scared of failing."

"These are concerns many students have when they go away to school. I know it doesn't feel like it, but it's a normal reaction. It'll be tough at first, but you'll get used to it. You're in a different place than when you left the first time. You have a support system. You have your parents, your sister, and Ryan. You left your support system behind when you left here years ago. You're taking them with you this time. It will be a different experience. A good one."

"Will you set me up with a therapist in San Diego?"

"Of course," she said, smiling. "If that's what you want. Or, you and I can still talk on the phone or do video calls. I have some clients I talk to over Skype. We can keep regular appointments that way, until you get acclimated. But you may find that when it's time to go, you don't need these appointments anymore."

"I doubt that," I mumbled.

"I don't. I think that come July, you'll be sick of me, if not long before that."

I shrugged, not knowing what to say. I didn't exactly want to tell Dr. Matson that I wanted to shrink her so I could keep her in my pocket forever. Deep down, I knew I was getting better. I knew I was almost entirely back to my old self. I was enjoying life again, something I hadn't been able to do since the shooting.

I shut my eyes tight. *The shooting.* Maybe that was my last hurdle.

"I think I need to talk about the shooting."

"What would you like to say?" Dr. Matson's face registered no shock or surprise, even though my statement came straight out of left field. In every session, I skirted around the reason I ended up in therapy in the first place. I never wanted to talk about it and always shut her down when she tried.

"I'm never going to forget that day, you know?" She nodded. "But I want to be able to not shut down when it crosses my mind."

"Does it cross your mind a lot?"

"Not as much as it used to since I've been keeping myself busy, but I still think about it sometimes. Especially when I'm going to bed at night. It's like it waits until there's nothing else on my mind to swoop in and take over."

"Any memories in particular?"

"Faces...the fear on people's faces. The loud bangs of the shots. The...the blood and the screams." The screams were the new worst. It used to be the faces of those who perished, the ones I'd seen alive before the shots rang out. The barista and the mom...I saw them less and less. I mostly heard the screams.

"What do you usually do to make those things go away?"

I considered her question. What *did* I do?

"Nothing really...I guess I just fall asleep. I don't know. I just wish..." I felt so guilty for my wish I couldn't even voice it.

"Go on."

"I wish it would go away...I wish it would all go away. I feel guilty for that."

"Guilty?"

"Yeah. People lost their lives, lost loved ones, lost the use of their legs, and here I am sitting here wishing I could stop seeing their faces and hearing their screams. Isn't that selfish? Because it feels selfish."

"It's not selfish, Anna. It's not selfish to want control of your mind back. You won't ever forget those things, but with time, you'll have the final say as to when you remember

133

them."

"You'll help me?" Hope colored my voice for the first time during our hour.

"We'll work on it," she said.

It wasn't a promise, but it would do.

***

After returning home from my appointments with Dr. Matson, I was drained. Mentally and physically sapped. My mind and body felt like they'd just participated in a marathon—no, a decathlon. Muttering an incoherent greeting to my parents and Ronnie, I hustled up the stairs to my bedroom and shut the door.

I needed *him.*

Sitting at my desk, I tapped the spacebar incessantly to wake up my computer. I'd need to replace it before I left for school. I opened my email, hoping to see the little green icon beside his name indicating he was online.

It wasn't there.

Of course it wasn't there. Ryan was in the military. He was somewhere—most likely in the middle of an ocean—and he was working. He wasn't available twenty-four-seven. We'd been lucky a few times, being online at the same time, but it was never a planned occurrence. It was luck. Pure luck.

I leaned back in my chair and sighed.

Dr. Matson and I had talked a lot about my feelings surrounding the shooting, and I was still too raw. I should have felt lighter, having purged all those thoughts and fears, but I didn't. I felt heavier...exposed...like I was wearing all those thoughts on the outside of my body.

I wanted to talk to Ryan because I knew

he'd make me feel lighter. He'd make me feel like everything would eventually be okay. He'd make me feel optimistic.

Technically, it was his turn to email me, but I composed a new message to him instead.

To: Ryan Jacobs
From: Anna Romano
Subject: Missing you.

Dear Ryan,
I had a rough day today. I talked to Dr. Matson about the shooting. Remembering what I saw, heard, and felt was difficult. All those memories are running rampant in the forefront of my mind, like they've finally been freed from the vault I'd kept them in. I want to tuck them away again. I don't want to remember anymore. I thought it would help me, but I'm not sure it has. Things have been going so well, the outlook of my life has been positive, and now I fear this has set me back. I went into my appointment today feeling afraid...anxious...about my future, about taking all these steps. I thought talking about the shooting would help, like it was the final puzzle piece, you know? The final thing holding me back from moving forward. It didn't quite work that way, though. I just needed to talk to you. To vent. You always knew the right things to say, even when I didn't want to hear them. Especially when I didn't want to hear them.
Love,
Anna

~ **22** ~

Ryan

I slammed my body down on my rack, a little surprised the flimsy bunk didn't crash to the floor with the force of my weight.

"Lady troubles?" Rogers mocked from his rack directly above mine.

"Fuck off," I muttered, knotting my hands behind my head. He had no idea how right he was.

My day was total and utter shit. Well, that wasn't entirely true. It started off alright, but it's amazing how that shit could change in the blink of an eye.

In the almost three years since I'd known Kelsey, she'd never pissed me off. Not once. She did today.

My daughter's face filled up the computer screen, lighting up my world. "Hey princess."

"Hi, daddy," she grinned with two fingers in her mouth.

"What did you do today?"

She proceeded to tell me about her time at day care in the most animated way. Her pretty blue eyes were bright, and she smiled that toothy grin I loved so much, absorbing me in her story about pink Legos and a princess castle. She was everything that was right in the world...she was my world.

As usual, she got distracted by something and took off for another part of the apartment.

Kelsey's image took over the screen. "How are things going?"

"Good, almost at the halfway point."

"That's great. How's Anna?"

I loved that Kelsey asked about Anna. It told me that things would be alright one day, when the two different parts of my life merged into one.

"She's good. She's applied to Braddock. There's a chance she might get in this fall, but it's a small chance."

Kelsey shifted in her seat and looked away from the screen. A sense of foreboding washed over me. What wasn't she saying?

"Kels?" I prompted.

She let out a sigh and looked back at the screen, her face showing signs of concern. "I think it's great that she's doing well, Ryan. I really do. But aren't things moving a bit...fast?"

"What do you mean?" I asked, sitting up straighter.

Kelsey shrugged. "She's still in therapy, right? Is she going to be healed by the time she gets to Braddock?"

"What are you getting at?"

"You know I respect you as a co-parent, Ryan. You're an amazing father, you provide for Charlotte—for me—more than I'd ever expected and more than I'd ever ask...but you haven't even told Anna about us yet. Not only that, I'm concerned..." she trailed off.

"Concerned about what?" I asked, skipping over the part about me not telling Anna about her and Charlotte. It wasn't exactly something I wanted to tell Anna over an email or online chat. I'd decided to talk to her face-to-face.

Kelsey glanced away again, struggling with whatever words were about to come out of her mouth. "I'm concerned about Anna being around Charlotte."

My jaw dropped. She was worried about Anna with Charlotte? Anna was a marshmallow, there was nothing to be concerned about. "Why? Why are you concerned? That doesn't even make sense."

"I figured you'd say that. I don't expect you to understand, Ryan," she said, shaking her head. "I don't want to fight with you about this."

"So don't."

"Ryan," she scolded, using the mom tone I'd often heard her use on Charlotte. "Think about it from my perspective, okay? This girl was your high school sweetheart, then the shooting happened and she became...unbalanced."

"She was depressed," I interrupted. "Probably had PTSD. That's not her fault."

"Of course it's not her fault," Kelsey added in a rush. "I'm not saying it is. It's just that she disappeared for years, and suddenly she's back. She's in therapy, which is great, and you guys are talking again, which is also great." She stared me right in the eyes, and I saw the ugly truth in them. "But I'm concerned about her being in San Diego so soon. If she's here, then there's no doubt she'll be in your life, which means she'll be in Charlotte's life. As a mom, I worry about that. What if she's still off balance? What if something were to trigger a memory or something and something bad happens when she's around Charlotte?"

"Jesus, Kelsey. That's what you're concerned about? You have nothing to worry

about. Anna is harmless."

"You don't know that," she whispered.

"I do know that."

"No," she said firmly. "You don't. You only see pieces of her, Ryan. What she wants you to see. What if she still has down times and just doesn't share them with you?"

"She wouldn't do that," I said, shaking my head. Anna wouldn't hide that kind of thing from me.

"You've spent years apart, Ryan. You don't know that."

"And you don't know her," I shouted, causing her to flinch. "I'm sorry..."

"Ryan, it's fine if you want to see Anna when she comes to San Diego. But I'm not ready for her to meet Charlotte."

"Excuse me?" My brows creased as the shock of her statement rolled through my system. I couldn't believe she was pulling that crap.

"Until I feel comfortable, I don't want her to be around Charlotte."

"You've got to be kidding me," I muttered, shocked at her words.

"I'm sorry, Ryan. I don't ask you for much."

"She's my daughter, too."

"I never said she wasn't. As a parent, I don't think it's smart to bring someone with a recent history of mental illness around my child. I'm honestly surprised you don't feel the same way."

I barked out a cold laugh. "That's because you don't know her."

"And you're blinded by your past with her...your present. You're not thinking like a father. You're thinking like a boyfriend."

139

My eyes snapped to hers. "I always have Charlotte's best interests at heart."

"You haven't even told Anna about Charlotte! You haven't told the woman you're falling in love with that you have a daughter. The woman who has a history of instability. You're going to rock her world when you tell her all that. Did you think about that, Ryan? Did you think about what your lies are going to do to her mental health?"

My fists clenched under the table. I thought about that every goddamned day. I didn't need Kelsey to remind me.

"Ryan, I don't want to fight. That's not why I brought this up. I just want you to consider another perspective. You can't tell me that if I met a man, you wouldn't be giving me the third degree about him, that you wouldn't be sitting at my kitchen table, cleaning your shotgun when he came to pick me up. We're friends Ryan, best friends. We look out for each other, and, together, we're supposed to look out for our girl. I'm just trying to get you to see things from my perspective because I think yours might be a little cloudy these days. That's all."

I'd never been so pissed at Kelsey, but more than that, I was pissed at myself because it was her right to be concerned. And she was damn right that I'd have any guy she ever dated vetted until there was nothing I didn't know about him, right down to his shoe size and where his grandparents went to elementary school.

I was confident Anna wouldn't be a danger to Charlotte, but I was a danger to Anna. All because I was too afraid to tell her about Charlotte in the first place. Kelsey was right, yet again. How much harm would it do to Anna when I finally told her about my daughter?

To make matters worse, when I abruptly ended the video call with Kelsey, there was an email waiting for me from Anna and she sounded...not right. She'd had a rough day and she needed me and I wasn't there. I looked for her chat icon, but she wasn't online.

I'd succeeded in failing two of the most important people in my life in one night.

The day couldn't end any fucking sooner.

~ 23 ~

Anna

As weeks passed, I felt better. The heaviness of the session with Dr. Matson lifted, and I started seeing the world in color again. We still touched on the shooting here and there, and it was easier. The pain and fear were still there, but they weren't nearly as crippling.

I received a frantic email from Ryan in response to the message I'd sent him after that session. I felt terrible for making him worry. I'd just felt stripped bare, and I didn't even think about how my words would affect him. I assured him I was okay, and after a fun and flirty video chat the following night, he believed me.

Dr. Matson told me I'd still have good days and bad days. That it was normal. Everyone had bad days, and my bad days didn't mean the sky was falling. She called it catastrophic thinking, and we spent three whole sessions talking about negative cognitions.

In one month, I'd be leaving for San Diego, the sixth of July. I wouldn't move into the dorms until August, but there were orientation activities in July, and I wanted to spend some time getting familiar with the campus and its surrounding area. My mother had a cousin who lived in Carlsbad, and I would be staying with her and her family until I could move into the dorm.

Relief flooded through me when I learned I'd have family close by. I only met Mom's cousin Mary a few times as a child, and I didn't remember her at all, but she was family and that was enough for me. I'd have her, her husband, their two kids, and, eventually, I'd have Ryan. I no longer feared being all alone on the other side of the country. I had people. A support system.

One rainy afternoon, Mom took me and Ronnie to Target to stock up on dorm essentials. I insisted on choosing a color scheme—dark blue, like Ryan's eyes—and my bedding, but I let them have their fun with everything I just had to have—their words, not mine. I had to admit, it was kind of nice to be spoiled, and I was having a fun girls' day out.

"Your dorm room better be on the ground floor," Ronnie said. She scrutinized two nearly identical throw pillows, first bringing one up to her face, then the next, alternating rubbing her cheeks against them like a cat. A strange one, my sister.

"I made the request, but I'm just a freshman, Ron. I don't have much pull."

"You have a handicapped sister, they should grant you a first floor room. How else am I going to see your room when I visit?"

"I don't know...take the elevator?" I ventured.

"What if the elevator is down? What if there is an earthquake or something? That's not safe."

"I'm pretty sure nowhere is safe when there is an earthquake. Besides, the San Andreas Fault doesn't run through San Diego."

"No, but a big one could hit and break off a chunk of California—the chunk with San Diego—and send you out to sea." I rolled my eyes, only Ronnie would come up with something that ridiculous.

"Have you started reading dystopian fiction, Ronnie?" I asked, smirking as I tossed a set of sheets that matched the navy and cream comforter I picked out into the basket.

"No," she sulked, throwing both pillows back on the shelf. "I'm going to miss you. I just got you back, and now you might fall into the ocean."

It was hard to be snarky now that I had a lump in my throat. My sister was ridiculous, but she was my ridiculous and this was her version of a deep conversation. "I'm going to miss you, too. You know you can come visit me whenever you want."

"Yeah...because it's easy to ship this much awesome," she gestured to her chair, "across the United States whenever I get a whim to see my little sis."

"You are pretty awesome."

She shrugged her shoulders. "I know."

"I'll come home for breaks and the entire summer."

"Pish. You say that now, but once you get there, and you and Ryan are all lovey-dovey again, you'll forget we even exist back here."

I paused my perusing and looked at her, my jaw slack. "Is that what you really think?" She shrugged her shoulders again, avoiding my gaze. I squatted down, resting on my haunches and placing my hands on her knees. "Ronnie, I'm never going to forget about you. You are my *best* friend. I don't know what's going to happen with Ryan, but it's not going to erase you from my life. I probably won't see him much anyway since he's always so busy. We'll Skype and email and talk on the phone...you're going to be sick of me."

One corner of her mouth tipped up. "We'll still have our book meetings?"

I nodded enthusiastically. "Heck, yeah. We might have to adjust the schedule depending on my classes, but we're definitely still meeting up to talk books."

She met my eyes and the lump in my throat grew at the sight of tears. "You're my best friend, too, Anna."

A tear slipped down my cheek as I leaned in to hug her. She held me tightly, and after a moment, we both laughed at our ridiculousness.

"Gosh, quit being such a baby. It's not like you're moving to another country." I stood up, both of us still laughing as we wiped our cheeks.

"What's so funny over here?" Mom asked, coming around the corner of the aisle with a shaggy, navy blue area rug rolled up in a tight coil. I eyed her speculatively, and she said, "I thought this would be nice to put under your bed, so your feet hit something soft and warm when you get up in the morning."

"It's perfect," I agreed. She thought of everything.

Digging through the shopping cart, Mom took inventory of our loot. "Looks like we're good on the bedroom stuff. Let's hit the towels and grab some other bathroom accessories, then we'll head over to the laundry supplies. Do you need any appliances?"

"My roommate is going to bring the TV and vacuum, so I volunteered for the microwave and refrigerator."

"You talked to your roommate?" Mom asked, looking pleased that I communicated with the stranger I'd be spending the next several months with.

"Yes. Her name is Megan. She seems very nice."

"Is she an art major as well?" Ronnie asked.

"Graphic design," I answered.

"Where is she from? What's her family like?" Mom asked.

"Whoa, Mom, we talked for like ten minutes, basically making sure we didn't double buy stuff we can share. I didn't ask her for a genealogical report. She lives in Florida."

"Oh, how nice! She's from the east coast, too," Mom said. "You'll have someone to commiserate with about being so far away from home."

"Yeah, but Anna will have Ryan, too," Ronnie said, and I shot her a look. I hadn't shared with my parents that Ryan was going to be in San Diego.

"Ryan will be in San Diego?" Mom asked, her brows knitted.

"Yes, he got his orders, and he'll be going to San Diego when he gets back."

"Oh, how nice," she said, giving me a cautious smile. "Well, those towels aren't going to buy themselves." She turned on her heel and headed down the aisle, back in the direction she'd come from.

I immediately felt bad. I hadn't planned on withholding that little bit of information from her, I just didn't want her to get the wrong idea when I wasn't even sure what the *right* idea was.

"I'm sure I won't see him much. He's really busy," I said as I followed after her, echoing just what I'd told Ronnie earlier.

Ronnie snorted. "Right. Like he wouldn't make time for you." I pinched her arm. "Ouch," she said, scowling at me and rubbing the sore spot. "What was that for?"

"Will you cool it with the Ryan stuff," I whispered harshly, nodding my head towards our mom who was paces ahead of us and gaining distance.

Ronnie's eyes widened for a second, then she nodded. "Yeah, fine. Sorry. I wasn't thinking."

"It's all right. I'm just not ready for questions I don't know the answers to."

"Want me to do damage control?" she offered, and I loved her for it.

"No, I'm going to have to face the music eventually. I guess I'll talk to her about it tonight."

"Want to make cookies after?"

"Yeah...chocolate chunk."

"I'll go get the chocolate," she said and buzzed off, scooting over to the grocery section.

"How about a light blue?" Mom asked when I met her in the towel aisle.

I rested my head on her shoulder, and she leaned hers against mine. "Sounds perfect."

~ **24** ~

To: Anna Romano
From: Ryan Jacobs
Subject: What's up?

Anna,
It's been a few days since I've heard from you. I hope everything is OK. Have you sketched anything new? I'd love to see pictures. I miss seeing your work. I miss watching you draw, the way your eyebrows knit together and you bite your lower lip. Or, when you were really focused, your tongue would stick out the tiniest bit. It was adorable. I could watch you sketch for hours.

Talk to you soon, I hope.
Ryan

To: Ryan Jacobs
From: Anna Romano
Subject: RE: What's up?

Dear Ryan,
I'm sorry I haven't written. Just working on getting some things together. And yes, I have been sketching, too. I attached a few pictures.

You know what I miss? Watching you play flag football with your friends. I loved sitting on the grass of the middle school football field on the weekends and watching you guys. Especially when you were on the skins team. Of course, I didn't like how the morning dew would get my butt all wet when I'd forget to bring a towel or blanket to sit on.

Do you ever talk to those guys? Mitch and Jordan? You guys were so close in high school. I haven't seen them around since I've been home. I haven't really seen anyone around, come to think of it. I guess I don't really hang out where people our age would hang out. The only places I really go are to the soup kitchen and Dr. Matson's office.

I still miss you. Every day. Even when I'm not writing.

Love,
Anna

To: Anna Romano
From: Ryan Jacobs
Subject: RE: RE: What's up?

Anna,
Ha, I remember you whining about your wet ass. Especially the time you wore those tiny little white shorts over the white panties with red dots on them. Clown Butt. Hilarious. One of my most favorite

149

memories.

The last time I talked to Mitch and Jordan was when I was home on leave a couple years ago. They went away to school and I enlisted, so we were all pretty busy, and it wasn't easy to keep in touch. One of us would touch base with the others when we knew we were going to be home, but it didn't always work out that we were in the same place at the same time. Then, my parents started coming to me when I had leave, since they were rarely ever at home anyway, so I went home less and less. A lot of people in our classes probably stayed wherever they went to school, or went where the jobs were in Charlotte or Raleigh. There isn't too much opportunity in Lakeside. Maybe you'll see some of them over Fourth of July if they come home to visit their families.

What kinds of things are you getting together? Still working on applications? Did you hear anything from Braddock?

Miss you, too.
Ryan

To: Ryan Jacobs
From: Anna Romano
Subject: Busy busy busy

Dear Ryan,
Yeah, I'm organizing stuff for school. Working on my portfolio and trying to figure

out what direction I want to go in. There are so many different focus areas, you know? I want to try to identify my weaknesses, so I can focus on building myself up in those areas. When I get to a school, I'm going to be surrounded by so much talent, I want to make sure I'm the best I can be. Kind of like how athletes train for games...maybe...I don't know, that's probably a stupid analogy.

I'll let you know if I see anyone over the holiday. I'm kind of nervous to see anyone I know, if I'm being honest. What if they think I'm a freak? Last they probably heard, I dropped out of high school and ran away from home. I don't really want to be in the spotlight, so I hope they either don't see me, or if they do, that they don't make a big deal out of it. Fortunately, we'll be on the boat, so we'll only see people at the dock.

And I'm totally ignoring the clown butt comment. That is not funny. That was mortifying. ALL the guys saw my panties that day and I don't remember having signed up for a wet shorts contest. I think my face was as red as the dots on my underwear. You know, I could always remind you of the time you were caught with your pants around your ankles!

So be nice.

Love,
Anna

PS No comment on the sketches?

To: Anna Romano
From: Ryan Jacobs
Subject: I'm unembarrassable.

Anna,
Shit, I forgot about the sketches. I'm sorry. I was so tired when I wrote you back last. I was so happy to see your response, I didn't want to wait to reply and I obviously wasn't thinking straight. The pictures were great. You do them in black and white, but I swear I can see them as though they are in color. I can picture the scenes perfectly. The one of the boat on the lake with the fireworks in the sky...those are some of my favorite memories. I always loved laying on the bow of the boat, with you in my arms, watching the fireworks. Those are some special memories, Anna.

And your analogy isn't stupid. Everyone needs to hone their talents, it's how they get better. It makes complete sense for you to be working on the things you feel are your weak areas. Of course, I don't believe you have any weak areas. You're a brilliant artist, and I know you're going to kick ass at whatever you do.

Don't worry about the people from school. You know Ronnie will take them down a notch if they dare say anything negative to you. She'll have your back. But really, what would they say? They all know what

152

happened, baby. They wouldn't blame you for checking out for a little bit. They'll see you now and see how strong and gorgeous you are and there won't be anything bad for them to say. You were well loved in high school, there's no reason they'd treat you poorly. They'd probably just be happy to see that you're back and you're OK.

And I dare you to bring up my pants incident. I'm unembarrassable, Anna.

Ryan

To: Ryan Jacobs
From: Anna Romano
Subject: That's not a word.

Ryan,
Unembarrassable is not a word. It's not even a thing. And you getting caught with your pants around your ankles in the boys' bathroom by Mr. Fisher because you found a freckle on your...member...was one of the funniest things on the planet. The look on your face when you came out with Mr. Fisher's hand on your arm as he escorted you to the principal's office. Hilarious. I can't believe he thought you were, you know, in the bathroom at school. I mean, your girlfriend was waiting right outside the bathroom! What kind of sense did that make?! About as much sense as you being fascinated by your penile freckle, that's how much. LOL!

Do you still have it?

Curious,
Anna

To: Anna Romano
From: Ryan Jacobs
Subject: Curiosity killed the cat.

Anna,
I don't really think it's appropriate for you to be curious about my penile freckle, as you so aptly called it. I guess you'll just have to see for yourself. And I can make up words if I want to, it's my right as an American. Freedom of speech.

There's something I want to talk to you about when I get home. It's nothing bad, it's actually really good. I don't want you to be nervous because it's nothing to be nervous about. I just want you to know that I want to tell you. I've wanted to tell you for a while now, but it's something I want to say to you in person.

I want to hug you right about now. So badly. I miss holding you. I miss touching you. I loved the way your soft skin would feel under my fingertips. And your smell, I really miss your smell. Like sugar and vanilla. Might be why I love sugar cookies so much.

I miss you more and more each day. It's crazy because every day is one day closer to seeing you, so it seems like some of the pressure on my chest should be lifted with each day, but it just makes me more eager…more anxious to see you.

If you can't come to San Diego until next fall, or if you end up at another school, we'll figure something out, A. I promise. I don't want to let you go again.

Love,
Ryan

~ 25 ~

Anna

A myriad of emotions flowed through me as I read Ryan's last email.

Guilt.

Joy.

Nervousness.

Love.

Yearning.

More guilt.

Anxiety.

I couldn't help but zero in on his closing...*love.*

Did that mean he still loved me?

I miss you more and more each day.

I don't want to let you go again.

Swoon.

Was I wrong for not telling him about San Diego? It wasn't wrong if it was a surprise, right? A good surprise? I didn't think so. I couldn't wait to surprise him. I was going to jump right into his big, strong arms. Maybe I'd even kiss him. I blushed at the thought alone. Was I that bold? After all, we had done much, much more than kiss in the past. Yet I still felt like it was the beginning all over again. A new beginning.

I spent a good thirty minutes worrying over what he wanted to talk to me about. Was it something that would hurt me? Did he want to stay friends? He said it wasn't bad, but that was his opinion. If he didn't see me as more than a friend, then he wouldn't think it was bad news at all. But his words...they weren't the kind of words you said to a friend. Did he want to get back together? Was I ready for that? Did it even matter since I was completely head over heels for him again? I could lie to Ronnie, and to my parents, but I couldn't lie to myself. I loved Ryan. I loved him, and I wanted to be with him.

Dr. Matson told me it was up to me if I thought I was ready to be in a relationship, and I didn't think she would have said that if she thought it was a bad idea. She was supposed to encourage me to take the lead role in my own life, but she had a particular tone she used when she thought I was going in the wrong direction. I called her out on it once, and she just gave me a little shrug and changed the subject. Yeah...I was on to her.

So was I ready to jump?

Heck, yeah...I was ready to hop, skip, jump, and dive right in!

I couldn't wait to be reunited with Ryan.

***

It rained the morning of the Fourth, and I was certain the holiday festivities would be cancelled. I should've known better. The weather in the Piedmont region of North Carolina was positively bipolar. Massive, hail producing thunderstorms one moment, sunny skies the next. By 11:30, we were on track for a beautiful afternoon on the lake.

Dad had left for the landing ahead of us to ready the boat. Mom, Ronnie, and I arrived shortly after noon. We had a picnic lunch on the boat, anchored near the shore of Rose Lake where the fireworks would be launched.

157

The four of us laughed, joked, and played games. We had a great time. The only thing missing was Ryan, and I was hyper-aware of that fact. Dad bought the boat the year Ryan and I had started dating in high school. There wasn't a summer on the lake that Ryan wasn't part of. Until now.

"You miss him," Ronnie said. It wasn't a question. She knew me too well. The memories of past summers with Ryan were hers, too.

"It's not the same without him. Don't get me wrong," I quickly added, "I'm having a great time with you and mom and dad."

"But it's different without him here. I get it. It's been like that for me, too. The last couple years out here...without you and Ryan...totally different. Dad would bring clients to entertain, but it royally sucked."

A pang of sadness and guilt had me reaching for my sister's hand and giving it a squeeze. "I'm sorry, Ron."

She squeezed my hand in response. "It's okay, Anna. We're here now."

We laid side by side on the bow, the gentle waves of the lake swaying the boat slightly. My head was tipped to face Ronnie, hers was tilted to face mine. I smiled at my sister, relishing those final few days I'd get to spend with her before I moved to California.

One moment, I was lying there with my sister.

The next...

The next moment I was back in Lakeside Mall.

On the floor, curled tightly into myself. My hands were wrapped around the back of my head and neck.

The only thing missing was Ryan.

He wasn't there to protect me this time.

~ 26 ~

Ryan

"I'll be down in a minute," I told Rogers as I slipped into the coms room.

We were meeting Gordon and Chambers for poker, but I hadn't gotten a message from Anna since before the Fourth of July, and I was worried. I thought she was distancing herself from me before, but she'd said she was just busy with college stuff. I believed her, I didn't have any reason not to. But three days had passed since her last message. I sent her two messages, and she didn't respond to either of them. If there wasn't a message from her in my inbox, I was reaching out to Ronnie. Enough was enough. I wasn't letting her push me away. Not again.

I logged online and pulled up my email.

Nothing.

Well, nothing from Anna, but there *was* an email from Ronnie marked as urgent.

Dread filled me. Why would Ronnie be messaging me? Why now? Why after three days of no contact from Anna?

Shit.

Clicking the message, I braced myself for bad news as I waited for it to open.

To: Ryan Jacobs
From: Veronica Romano
Subject: Urgent!

Ryan,
Please call me on Skype as soon as you can. It's for Anna and it's important. Please.
Ronnie

Wasting no time, I closed the email window and logged onto Skype. Ronnie and I had talked on Skype before, so I clicked her name and called her right away.

"Ryan, thank God," Ronnie said as soon as the call connected. I couldn't see her, the room she was in was completely dark. I knew it was late there, maybe 9:30. She must have flipped a switch, because a dim light suddenly filled the room behind her. Anna's room.

"What's going on?" Ronnie sighed. She looked exhausted. Exhausted and defeated. "Is Anna okay?"

"Everything was fine. We were having a great day at the lake. Anna was her old self again, laughing and joking and playing games. We were lying on the bow of the boat talking, waiting for the fireworks to start, then all of a sudden she was curled up in a ball and freaking out." Tears spilled down Ronnie's cheeks as she recalled what happened. "She's back in that place, Ryan."

Fuck. I couldn't let her go back there...I couldn't lose her again.

My mind raced back to that day. That horrible day I went to surprise my girlfriend at the mall. She'd been there to help Ronnie pick out a prom dress. I'd needed new sneakers, so I decided to hijack their girls' day.

After spending almost an hour of trying on different pairs of cross trainers, I finally gave up and left the shoe store. I ordered a large lemonade from the stand outside the store. I loved fresh lemonade; it was all about the pulp. Anna hated pulp.

Anna.

I couldn't wait to see her. I just saw her the night before, but it was never enough. The best part about it? She felt the same way. We couldn't get enough of each other. It was hot. She *was hot.*

I paid for my drink and headed to the spot in the food court where Anna texted she'd be. I was eager to get my hands on my girl. As I rounded the final corner, dining tables in sight, a gun shot rang out, echoing off the glass and marble.

People began screaming and running, bumping into me as they fled the area. My survival instincts kicked in, and my brain told me to run, too.

But I had only one thing on my mind...Anna.

I ran towards the chaos, looking across the wide space, trying to spot her.

There she was, standing right in front of the coffee shop, exactly where she said we'd meet. She was frozen in place, glass shattering beside her. She didn't even flinch. Shock had frozen her body.

"Get down," I yelled, but she couldn't hear me.

It felt like hours went by, but in reality, it hadn't even been a minute since the first shot rang out.

Seconds later, I collided with Anna and brought her down to the ground. She fought me, yelling incomprehensibly through her tears. I whispered in her ear, telling her I'd keep her safe over and over until she finally relaxed in my arms.

I'd been too late that day. The damage had already been done, and Anna would never be the same. As well as she may seem, that terrified girl from the mall was still inside her.

It wasn't difficult to deduce that the sound of the fireworks sent Anna right back to that day at the mall. I never experienced PTSD firsthand, but you heard enough about it in the military. Everyone either knew a guy or knew a guy who knew a guy.

"Let me see her," I told Ronnie. "I want to talk to her."

Ronnie nodded. "That's why I emailed you. I think you might be the only one to pull her out of this. Dr. Matson has been by, but Anna wouldn't talk to her. She just lays in her bed, either sleeping or staring at the wall. I just got my sister back--" Ronnie's soft sobs cut her off. She must have set her iPad on her lap because I was getting a view of the ceiling fan as she rolled her chair to Anna's bedside.

I heard some rustling and the iPad moved around before it stilled. She must have propped the tablet against something because I was soon looking right at her sleeping face. Her head was resting on her pillow, and I could see her anguish, even in sleep. She looked tortured.

"Anna," Ronnie called out softly. "Open

your eyes." Anna's eyes fluttered but stayed shut. "Ryan's on the phone."

"Hey, baby," I said, and her eyes slowly popped open, glassy with tears.

"Ryan," she whispered.

"Hi."

A few big tears slipped from her eyes as she gazed blankly at me. "I was so scared," she said, her voice so low I could barely hear her. "I was so scared, and you weren't there."

Fuck.

That gutted me.

"I know, baby. But I'm here now. Talk to me."

"I heard the gunshots. I called for you, but you didn't come. I covered my head like you did. I was so scared."

"Baby, you know it wasn't really gunshots, right? You weren't at the mall. You were on the boat with your parents and Ronnie. The sound you heard, it was fireworks."

Her eyebrows scrunched together like she couldn't quite believe what I was telling her. It would have been cute if she wasn't so damn wrecked. I wanted to be laying on that bed beside her with my arms wrapped around her.

"Baby, you had a flashback. The fireworks were loud and reminded you of the sound of the gunshots, but it wasn't real." She shook her head, and I nodded in return.

"No," she argued. "It was real."

"I know it seemed that way, but it wasn't real. It was in your head."

"I didn't make it up," she snapped.

"I know you didn't. It's just a memory, Anna. It doesn't mean it wasn't real, it just wasn't real the other day." She shook her head again, her expression disbelieving. "Have I ever lied to you, Anna?" I asked, cursing myself as I thought of my daughter and the truth I hadn't shared with Anna.

"No," she replied in a small voice.

"I'm not lying to you now."

Her eyes searched mine, they looked for the truth. I saw the moment she found it, her entire being sagging in defeat.

"I thought I was better," she whimpered, the tears flowing again.

"You *are* better, Anna. You are. There may always be things that remind you of that day. You need to let Dr. Matson help you. She's helped you with a lot of other things, she'll help you with this, don't you think?"

Anna nodded, and I exhaled a breath in relief.

We were not losing her to her mind again. Not this time.

"It's late; why don't you go to sleep and go see Dr. Matson in the morning?"

"Okay," she said, her voice quiet. She looked down, away from the screen. I got the feeling she was holding something back. I didn't want us to hold anything back anymore.

"What is it?" I asked. Her eyes darted to mine. "I know you, baby. What aren't you saying?"

She glanced behind me—well, behind the iPad—to where I guessed Ronnie still sat.

"I'm going, I'm going," I heard Ronnie say.

Anna looked down again, and I waited. I wouldn't rush her. Not now.

Then, she looked into my eyes with

165

complete clarity and said, "I love you."

I couldn't help the grin that spread across my face. "I love you, too, baby. I love you so much."

She smiled, and I decided I'd never get sick of seeing her smile. Ever.

"Go to bed, A. Get some sleep and we'll talk tomorrow, okay?"

She nodded. "Good night, Ryan."

"Good night, gorgeous."

I disconnected and the call window disappeared. I was still grinning at the computer like an idiot, though, and I imagined that wouldn't change anytime soon.

"That was some pretty serious shit," Rogers said, and I jumped a good foot off the chair.

"What the fuck, man?" I asked, swiveling the chair around to face him.

"Sorry," he said, holding his hands up in front of him. "I came to see what the hell was taking you so long. I didn't want to interrupt."

"So you just watched?" I asked, pissed as hell at him. I turned back to the computer and shut it down, then stood and confronted him, crossing my arms in front of my chest.

"You love her?" He asked, ignoring my question.

"I always have."

"She's pretty. Prettier than that picture you keep in your wallet."

"What the hell are you doing in my wallet?" I asked, appreciating that he wasn't going to try to get into the heavy stuff he'd overheard.

"How do you think I pay for half the pizzas I order at home?"

"Asshole," I muttered, pushing past him

and out to the hall. He was hot on my trail.

"She gonna be okay?" he asked after a moment.

"I hope so."

"I didn't realize...when you said you were talking to her again I got kind of pissed. I thought you were an idiot to open that box back up again after what she did to you, but I think I get it now."

"Oh yeah?"

"Yeah," he said, nodding his head. "Look, man, we don't do this heart to heart shit. It's not our style. But that's some heavy shit, and if you ever need to talk about it, I'm here. Can't have all that bogging you down. You need an outlet, you come to me."

A tip of my chin let him know I understood what he was saying, and we didn't speak about it again. I appreciated that my brother was there if I needed him, but we weren't about to hug it out or anything.

We met Gordon and Chambers in the lounge and spent the next couple hours playing poker for pretzels.

~ 27 ~

Anna

California was beautiful—everything I'd ever expected and more—if that was even possible. I took a long road getting there, literally and figuratively, but I made it, albeit six weeks later than I'd planned due to my mental regression. I was absolutely in love with my new home.

The day after I'd talked to Ryan, I went to see Dr. Matson, who immediately put me through intensive exposure therapy. In short, it was a crash course in dealing with loud noises without turning into a shriveling mess. It was the worst four weeks of my life, but it was necessary. I'd probably still be hiding in my bedroom at home if it wasn't for the therapy. My reaction was completely unexpected, I hadn't displayed many anxiety symptoms since the shooting—nothing had triggered that kind of reaction in me before. My symptoms were centered on depression, so that's where Dr. Matson focused my therapy. Sure, I'd jump when a door slammed, or if there was a loud bang, but who didn't? I'd never experienced a sound as loud as the fireworks...so closely resembling the gunshots. I didn't know that would happen, and I felt horribly guilty for putting my family through that. It made it even more difficult for them to leave me here in California, I was sure of that.

Which is probably why Mom was spending the week with her cousin and hadn't gone home yet.

I ended up arriving in San Diego just in time to move into the dorms with the other freshmen. At the moment, I was sitting on my freshly made twin bed, waiting for my roommate to arrive. We'd emailed, but hadn't met yet, and I was looking forward to meeting Megan.

As if I'd conjured her with my thoughts alone, the dorm room door swung open and a tall brunette with a big smile was standing before me. She was dressed in pale pink capri pants, a white t-shirt, and white sandals. Her tan looked like she spent the entire summer on the beach. She was gorgeous, and I suddenly felt so ordinary in my denim shorts, graphic tee, and black Chucks.

"Anna?!" She exclaimed in her sweet—and slightly high-pitched—voice. *That would take some getting used to.*

"Megan?" I asked, standing up. I brushed the front of my shorts, smoothing them out. A nervous habit.

"The one and only! It's so good to meet you. Gosh, you're gorgeous." She dropped her bags on the floor and threw her arms around my neck.

Okay. She was a hugger. I could handle that. I'd handled worse. And she thought *I* was gorgeous, another point for Megan, even if she needed glasses.

"I'm so excited," she squealed, stepping back, but keeping her hands on my shoulders.

"Are your parents here?"

"They're parking the car," she said, rolling her eyes. "I told them you and I had bonding time planned for lunch, so they won't stay after we unload."

"I don't mind," I told her. I missed my parents and sister already and they hadn't been gone but a few hours. I didn't want her to pass up time with her family just for me.

"They've been unnaturally clingy the past few weeks. I love them to pieces, but I need some me time." She looked around the room, taking in the decor Ronnie had helped me set up. Well, it was more like she directed, and I followed her instructions. I was glad I ended up with a first floor room to accommodate my sister.

"Sorry I went ahead and put everything up. My sister wanted to help."

"It looks great," she said, still smiling that beauty queen smile. She paused, noticing the frame on my nightstand and walked over, picking it up. "Who's this?"

It was a picture of me and Ryan from his graduation. He looked so handsome in his cap and gown, the shade of blue made his eyes the brightest I'd never seen them.

"That's Ryan. My boyfriend," I boldly added, knowing that even though we'd exchanged I love yous, we hadn't yet defined our relationship.

"He's hot. You look different here though. Was it taken a while ago?"

"Yes," I said, stepping over to where she was standing and taking the frame from her hands. Ryan's eyes sparkled up at me, and I grinned, missing his face. "It was his high school graduation. He's a year older than me.

He graduated six years ago." Before everything went to hell.

"That's right. I forgot you said you'd been out of high school a while. Five years, huh? That's a long time."

I could tell she was digging for info. I didn't know how much I wanted my new roommate to know about my past. Thanks to Dr. Matson, I was much less ashamed of my choices, but I also didn't want to freak Megan out on our first day together. Baby steps.

"Some things happened, and I needed some time is all." I set the frame back on the nightstand and gave her a shy smile, hoping she'd change the subject.

"You get knocked up or something?" Megan asked, startling me so much I barked out a laugh.

"What? No!"

She just shrugged. "So that means you're like...twenty three?"

"Twenty-two," I corrected, feeling a little self-conscious of the age difference. I was at least four years older than most of the students in the freshman class. That wasn't awkward...not at all.

Megan's grin stretched from ear to ear. "Awesome! You can buy all the alcohol!"

I rolled my eyes inwardly. Yeah...awesome.

Fortunately, before Megan could start writing down the list of her favorite types of alcohol, we were interrupted by her parents' arrival. She was in the middle of spouting off brands of liquor I had never heard of as it was. Yes, I'd had a few drinks here and there over the years—both before and after turning twenty-one—but it was usually when I'd sneak one of my dad's beers with Ryan or Ronnie, or drown in a cheap bottle of wine after a horrible day at one of the many diners I'd worked at through the years. I'd never tried fruit flavored vodka or cinnamon anything.

Megan's parents—Mr. and Mrs. Barstow—were kind, nurturing people. They reminded me so much of my own parents, it made me miss them all over again. It didn't seem like that little pang in my chest was ever going to go away. In the hour the Barstows were in our room unloading Megan's things, they must have told her they loved her and were proud of her at least twenty times. Megan didn't seem to appreciate their doting as much as I did, years of being away from my family did that to me, resulting in my appreciation of every moment with my parents.

Mr. and Mrs. Barstow left just before noon, promising to be back in a few hours to pick Megan up for dinner as they were taking a redeye back to Florida that evening. I could tell Megan's mother didn't want to leave her, but her dad insisted they see some of the city and let us girls have some bonding time.

"I thought they'd never leave," Megan sighed, falling onto her bed dramatically.

"I think they're sweet," I told her, sitting on the edge of my bed.

"They're okay. You ready to grab something to eat? I'm starving," she said, grabbing her stomach. I was surprised she wasn't studying drama with all her theatrics. This was going to be an interesting year.

"Yes. I passed a little café on the way in." I

stood up and grabbed my wristlet off my dresser.

"Sounds perfect." Megan rolled off her bed and lifted her beige leather bag off the floor. The thing was huge. I wondered what she had in it, but didn't feel comfortable asking, though I was sure Megan wouldn't mind. She'd probably dump the contents out all over her bed and offer me a perusal. She seemed very open.

Maybe we were placed together for a reason. Maybe the personality team in the housing department matched us up because she was the extrovert to my introvert. Megan would break me out of my shell, I was sure of it.

"I can't wait to hear all about your boyfriend," Megan sang as she strutted out the door.

I sighed as I followed her. This would be an interesting year for sure.

~ 28 ~

Anna

"He's in the Navy? That's so cool. I can't believe *my* roommate's boyfriend is in the military. Does he have abs? Does he have any hot friends? Do you think he can set me up with someone? Will you ask him? When does he get home? When can I meet him?"

Megan prattled on and on and on, barely stopping to take a breath. I wasn't sure if I was meant to answer her questions or not, since she wasn't giving me the opportunity to say anything.

Finally, she paused, and I looked up from my sandwich to see her looking at me expectantly. "I don't know if he has any hot friends. I'm not sure if he'll tell me if he does or not, but I guess I can ask. He gets home in October, and I guess you can meet him after that. He doesn't know I'm here yet. I'm surprising him."

"Oh! That's so romantic. This one time, my sophomore year boyfriend..." and she was off again. I couldn't keep up. Had I been that unsocial over the years that I couldn't have a girl-talk conversation anymore? Was this what conversations were like when I was in high school? I didn't remember talking at the speed of light. "So what do you think?" Megan asked, and I turned my gaze back towards her.

"About what? I'm sorry, I zoned out," I

admitted, heat rising in my cheeks.

"I bet you did. I'd zone out, too, if that hunk was my boyfriend." My entire face heated now. I hadn't been thinking about Ryan that moment, but he was never too far from my mind. "I asked if you wanted to swing by the registration tents and see if we can get appointments with our advisors."

"Yeah," I agreed, knowing I had to register for classes sooner rather than later in order to get into the ones I needed.

We paid our checks and ventured out into the warm, southern California air. It was a beautiful day, and according to my research, the weather was almost always this beautiful. Rain wasn't a common occurrence and snow didn't happen at all—my days of precipitation were over. I was used to all kinds of weather in Seattle; San Diego would be a cakewalk in comparison.

We walked back to campus and headed for the registration tents. The school was holding a fair of sorts for students, particularly freshmen, featuring tents and tables for different majors, clubs, and departments. It was pretty empty, since most students were still moving into the dorms, so we were able to sit down with our advisors right away.

After thirty minutes spent poring over the course catalog, I ended up enrolled in two courses for my major: drawing and two-dimensional design, two gen ed classes: English Composition and Algebra, and one elective: Introduction to Psychology. Maybe that last one would give me some insight into my own mind.

Megan met me outside the tent, having

completed her registration as well. We compared schedules on the way back to our dorm, realizing we'd have both English Comp and Psychology together. We looked at the rest of our days, and made plans to meet for lunch or dinner when our schedules would allow.

While she went out for dinner with her parents, I searched the web for jobs. My parents had told me not to worry about my expenses because they planned on sending me a monthly allowance, but I wanted to do something for me. I knew if I did nothing but go to school, I would have too much time on my hands to think about Ryan, and the next month and a half would drag.

I couldn't wait to see him again. We had been video chatting more this past month, but Skype just wasn't the same. Seeing his smile and hearing his laugh had been amazing though. I'd have to work something out so I could still video chat with Ryan without giving away my location or letting him see Megan.

I browsed the classified ads some more. A lot of restaurants were hiring, but I wasn't sure if I wanted to work in a restaurant. I had experience as a server, but I think I exhausted that particular form of employment in Seattle. I was one dissatisfied customer away from losing my cool.

"My steak is too tough." *Well, you ordered a well-done steak from a* diner*, what did you expect?* "My coffee is too hot." *Really?* "This ice cream is too cold." *You're kidding right?* "I'd like a salad with no tomatoes, cucumbers, carrots, croutons, or onions.

Dressing on the side." *So you'd like a bowl of lettuce?*

It was decided. Definitely no restaurants.

Skimming through some more ads, I was ready to give up when I spotted the magic words. Art gallery. A local art gallery was hiring for an assistant. I'd never worked in an art gallery before, but I was an art student. I must have been a little qualified. The ad was short and to the point; it didn't list any required experience, and I wasn't sure if that meant they were flexible, or that applicants should already know the kind of experience one would need to work as an assistant in an art gallery.

I didn't care. I picked up my cell phone and dialed the number.

"Martine's Fine Arts," a feminine voice sang across the line.

"Hello, I'm calling about the gallery assistant position."

"Do you have a resume?" the voice asked abruptly.

"I do," I answered. *Thank you college preparedness!*

"Send it over. We'll call for an interview if we're interested." She spouted off an email address and hung up, cutting off my "thank you."

Well, that seemed promising.

I logged in to my email, and sent my resume to the generic email address Miss Attitude gave me, including a cordial "To Whom It May Concern" message that would probably just get deleted. I also attached a couple of the scanned images I'd sent to Ryan, just for shits and giggles. I might not have had experience working in an art gallery, but I wasn't a complete idiot when it came to the arts. Maybe the two would balance each other out. Or maybe they wouldn't.

Only time would tell.

I closed out of my email and opened Skype. Ryan had been active fifteen minutes ago.

Dammit.

Forty-seven more days. I just had to make it forty-seven days and then I'd see him in person.

Exhausted after my busy day, I decided to forgo heading to the cafeteria for dinner and curled up in bed with a book. Looking at my alarm clock, I figured I still had an hour before Megan would return, bringing all her energy with her.

I fell asleep in the middle of chapter two, right after the heroine met the hero during their freshman orientation.

~ **29** ~

To: Ryan Jacobs
From: Anna Romano
Subject: 30 days!

Dear Ryan,
Sorry I missed your Skype call again. Maybe we can try to connect tomorrow?

Are you excited to be heading home soon? Will you go straight to San Diego, or do you have to stop in Virginia first?

I've been keeping busy sketching and building my portfolio. I'm attaching my latest here. I hope you like it.

Love,
Anna

To: Anna Romano
From: Ryan Jacobs
Subject: 25 days!

Anna,
Sorry, since we're on the home stretch, there's lots to do. I haven't been able to get as much computer time as I'd like. The sketch was gorgeous, just like you. Did you do that from memory? It looks just like the

179

picture of us from the homecoming dance. I bet you traced it. Ha-ha.

I do have to go back to Virginia, but only for a minute before I head to San Diego. I wish I could come see you in between, but I need to get to California and take care of some things. I'll have a week of leave after that, though, and I'd love to see you. If you can't come to me, I'll go to you. It's been too long. I wish I'd spent more time with you before I left.

It's kind of hard to plan our Skype calls. Maybe we should just wait until I'm home to see each other again. It'll make it that much more worth it. Anticipation and all that.

I'll see you soon.

Love,
Ryan

PS I know you didn't trace it. You are the most talented person I know.
PPS I love you.

To: Ryan Jacobs
From: Anna Romano
Subject: 21 days!

Ryan,
I like the idea of waiting to see each other again until we can actually see each other again. I feel all warm and fuzzy inside just thinking about it.

180

I love you, too.

I can't believe you accused me of tracing! I do not trace. I'm appalled you'd even suggest it. Even if you were kidding.

Just kidding.
Kind of.

Counting down the days,
Anna

To: Anna Romano
From: Ryan Jacobs
Subject: Two weeks!

Dear Anna,
In just two weeks I'll be docking in Virginia. I wish I could request a drop-off in North Carolina, but I think the Navy would frown upon a request from a sailor to be dropped off at his girlfriend's house. That's so high school. Kind of reminds me of our first date. My parents were out of town and you had to ask your dad to drive us. I never told you, but I was terrified of him. Seems kind of silly to even say now considering how close I've been with your family over the years, but yeah...you were my first girlfriend, so meeting your dad was kind of a big deal. I was afraid to hold your hand in the movie theater that night. I thought I'd turn around in my seat and he'd be sitting right behind us.

Anyway, I can't wait to see you.

Love,
Ryan

To: Ryan Jacobs
From: Anna Romano
Subject: LOL

Ryan,
Your message made me laugh so hard. What did you think my dad would be doing in the movie theater? Cleaning his gun? Hahahahaha. I don't even know what to say. That's so funny. I remember you being all tense, but I had no idea what was going through your mind. I thought it was just the usual first date jitters that made you avoid touching me like I was infected with the plague. No wonder I didn't get a good night kiss until our fifth date. You were scared. Of my dad. My dad is such a teddy bear, Ryan.

Thanks for making me laugh. I needed that.

Will you have time to call me when you get to Virginia? When is your flight to San Diego?

Love,
Anna

PS Your girlfriend?

To: Anna Romano
From: Ryan Jacobs
Subject: It wasn't that funny...

Anna,
I'm glad you find my teenage trauma so amusing. I didn't know if your dad had a gun. He could have. I was a fourteen year old boy, a stick figure, for crying out loud. He was your dad. He could have taken me out with his pinky if he wanted to. Now I know he's a big softy, but I didn't back then. I just saw him as a big, scary dad who would do anything for his daughter. You and Ronnie always have been his weaknesses. It's why you two always got away with so much shit.

I'll be in Virginia for a couple days wrapping things up with the ship and preparing to relocate. I can definitely call you when I get some time. I can't wait to hear your voice. I fly to San Diego on October 7th. My flight gets in around noon, California time. I'll call you when I get there, too. Then, once I talk to my CO, I'll let you know when my leave is and we'll work all that out.

Ten days, Anna. Just ten more days and I'll be back in the US. I wish that was the countdown to when I'll be seeing you, but at least I'll get to hear your voice.

Love,
Ryan

PS Yes, you're my girlfriend.

To: Ryan Jacobs
From: Anna Romano
Subject: 2 more days!

Dear Ryan,

I can't wait to hear your voice, boyfriend.

Love,
Anna

~ **30** ~

Ryan

Setting foot on dry land never got old. I loved being on the ship and doing my job, but I loved coming home even more. There was no place like the United States, not even the air craft carrier I'd spent the last several months on.

As my orders currently stated, I'd have thirty-six months shore side. It was exactly what I needed. I'd get to spend a lot of time with Charlotte, time she'd actually remember since she was getting to the age where she'd retain memories. I couldn't wait to make them with her.

Then there was Anna. I needed some time stateside to see if what we'd been building over email, chat, and video could really go somewhere. I loved her. There was no question about that. But would everything be as real in person as it was online? And there was also the fact that we were on opposite coasts. What if she didn't get accepted into Braddock? Then what? She'd have to go to school somewhere else; I wouldn't allow her to give up her dream just to be near me. I wasn't that selfish.

Rogers and I were sharing a hotel room for the few days we'd be in Virginia before leaving for California. He was out at a bar, which gave me a perfect, quiet opportunity to call Anna.

"Hey, beautiful," I said once the call connected.

"Ryan! I'm so happy it's you. I wasn't sure when you'd call."

"I called as soon as I could," I said. The excitement in her voice was palpable, and I found myself smiling.

"I'm so glad. How are you? How is it being back?"

"It's good. Different, but good. How are you?"

"I'm great. I'm just so excited to hear from you, I can't really think about anything else."

"I know the feeling. Any word from Braddock?" I asked, hoping she'd gotten good news. The fall semester was already underway, but maybe she'd get in for spring?

"I might have a little surprise for you, but you're going to have to wait for it."

"If it's a good surprise, I can definitely wait. So what else have you been up to? Tell me everything." I reclined on the stiff hotel bed, resting my head on the pillow as I listened to her tell me about her sketches and the books she's been reading. I frowned when she told me she interviewed for a job as an assistant at an art gallery, but I couldn't let my disappointment show because she was just so damn happy about it. It meant she was planning to stay in North Carolina, though. She wouldn't get a job and then move a couple months later. Not a job like that anyway.

"I really hope I get it. It would be so awesome to work in a gallery and be surrounded by art all day. The manager really loved the sketches I submitted with my application. I sent in a copy of the treehouse and the one of the roses in my parents' backyard. She was so impressed. We talked for about an hour about our favorite artists and stuff. I was a little worried since I have no gallery experience, but she didn't seem to mind at all. She just loves that I have a passion for art."

"That's great, baby. I'm happy for you."

"Thanks, Ry. It would just be part-time, which is totally fine. It'll get my foot in the door. And, now that they've seen my work, maybe they'll show it one day. I've been doing a lot of research and a lot of the art world is about networking. Even if I don't get the job, I might be able to use these connections years from now. How awesome is that?"

Her enthusiasm was infectious, and despite the fact I was selfishly bummed she wouldn't be going to San Diego anytime soon, I was happy for her. She needed this. She needed something to make her feel good and help solidify her place in this world. I knew she still struggled with her identity and her purpose from time to time. This would be a great opportunity for her.

"It's very awesome, A. You'll get the job, they'd be crazy not to hire you."

"You think?" Her unsure tone made me want to reach through the phone and hug her. If only...

"I know."

"Thanks, Ry. Gah! I've been babbling, and I haven't even let you speak at all. What are you doing?" God, she was adorable.

"Nothing much. Finished with work for the day so now I'm at the hotel."

"You must be exhausted."

"I am. I'm going to go to bed in a little while."

"Me, too. It's been a long day. Why don't you just go to bed now? I know I've been dying to talk to you, but if you're tired I'll feel terrible for keeping you awake. You can call me tomorrow after you've gotten some good rest in a real bed."

"Thanks, babe. I might do that. Just lying in this bed has me tired. I'll call you tomorrow, okay?"

"I'm so glad you're home, Ryan. I missed you."

"I've missed you, too. It's good to be home."

"I love you." She said the words slowly, carefully, as if she was simply trying them out.

"I love you, too," My tone left no room for misunderstanding. I loved her, and I was going to make sure she knew it.

"Good night, Ryan," she said, and the happy was back in her voice.

"Good night, A."

I disconnected the call and scrolled through my contacts. One more call to make before I could go to sleep. I tapped Kelsey's name on the screen and started a video call.

"Daddy!" Charlotte squealed, a moment later her image appeared.

"Hi, princess."

"You home?" she asked, tilting her head to the side and playing with a loose curl. Her hair was getting longer and longer. I bet she'd be a whole head taller when I saw her in San Diego in two days.

"Almost. I'm in Virginia. I'll see you the day

after tomorrow. Two more sleeps." She held up a hand and showed me two fingers. "That's right, baby girl. Two."

"I wuv you." Hearing those words out of her little mouth would never get old. Ever.

"I love you, too."

"Mommy want to talk to you," she said, and the phone shook as she toddled to wherever Kelsey was. "Hewe you go. Bye, Daddy."

"Bye, princess." The phone jerked some more before Kelsey appeared. "Kels," I greeted. She was still pissed at me, and I didn't blame her. I tried to apologize, but it didn't help that neither of us would budge on the Anna situation.

"Ryan."

I sighed, she wasn't going to make this easy. But then again, neither was I. I gave her my flight information, and after agreeing to bring Charlotte to the airport, she quickly ended the call.

I laid my head on my pillow and closed my eyes. Two more days until I saw my daughter. Another week or so until I saw Anna.

I was counting the seconds.

~ 31 ~

Anna

San Diego International Airport was a lot busier—and larger—than the airport back home. There were people everywhere and they were all moving with focused determination. I felt like I was in the way, even though I was standing off to the side in baggage claim.

At least I was entertained. A little girl with bouncing blonde curls was giving her mother a run for her money. She tried to climb onto one of the baggage carousels three times, her mother wrangling her away just in time, each time. The little girl was positively adorable, but her mother looked exhausted.

I was reading on my Kindle, waiting impatiently for Ryan's flight, when the little girl approached me.

"Hi wady. Watcha doin'?" I smiled at her little lisp and set my Kindle down on the empty seat beside me.

"I was reading a book. What are you doing?"

"Waitin' for my daddy," she said, curling her fingers in her hair.

She was absolutely precious. Her dark blue eyes were a familiar shade, and I smiled at how it must have been another sign I'd be seeing Ryan soon. I'd been seeing him in strangers all over the last couple days.

"I bet he's going to be excited to see you," I said. Her father was probably military; there were so many men and women in uniform bustling around the airport.

She nodded her little head. "He cawls me pwincess."

"You look just like a princess."

She gave me a big, toothy grin. "I know!"

Little kids were so modest. I couldn't even remember the last time I'd spent time around a small child. I never babysat as a teenager, and I didn't have any small cousins or anything. There were a few kids who would go to the soup kitchen with their parents, but they were so shy and skittish. Nothing like the little princess at the airport.

"Charlotte," her mother scolded, approaching us. "I'm so sorry," she told me, giving me an embarrassed smile as she took her daughter's hand.

"It's quite all right. I haven't ever been in the presence of a real princess before."

The woman laughed. "That she is. Her father spoils her rotten. I keep telling him he's going to give her a complex, but he doesn't listen. I feel terrible for the man she eventually marries."

"I gonna mawwy daddy!" Charlotte announced. Her mother shook her head while I laughed.

"He must be a prince in order to get to marry a princess," I said.

Her eyes widened, and she looked up at her mother. "Is daddy my pwince?"

"Yes, sweetheart. Your daddy is your prince." Charlotte smiled that toothy grin again and my heart melted. She was so sweet. "Come on, little one. Let's go check the board for Daddy's flight." She looked at me. "Sorry about that."

"She was no bother at all. She's very sweet."

"That she is," she smiled and they both gave me a small wave before they walked off to check the monitors on the other side of baggage claim.

I looked at my watch. Last time I checked, Ryan's flight was due to arrive on time at 12:05. It was 12:04.

My heart raced at the thought of seeing him again. Would he be happy to see me? I hoped he wouldn't be upset that I withheld the truth. It was just so much better this way. At least I thought it was. He did seem a little distracted when we spoke yesterday. He mentioned that *thing* he had to talk to me about again. My nerves were fried from anticipation. He seemed...off.

Well, hopefully seeing me would change his tune because it was almost go time. In just a few short minutes, he'd be walking through those doors to get his bags, and I'd be here, ready or not, waiting for him.

I tried to imagine it in my head. Would I run to him and jump into his open arms? Would he smile at me, then shake his head like he'd done all those times I'd tried to surprise him in the past. Like the time I threw him a surprise party for his eighteenth birthday. His parents had been out of town, so I snuck over to his house and invited a few of his buddies. He didn't get mad at me when he got home, he just smiled and shook his head, like he couldn't believe the things he let me get away with.

This would be just one more of those

things because he loved me.

He loved me, and I was his girlfriend again.

Whatever he had to tell me didn't matter because we'd be together again soon, and this time I wouldn't be so foolish and let him go. I'd never let him go again.

A canned voice came over the loudspeaker saying that the luggage for Flight 2056 would be arriving on carousel one.

If possible, my pulse sped up even more. I thought my heart would beat straight out of my chest. If his baggage was here, then *he* was here.

I stood on shaky legs and looked around, trying to catch sight of his tall, wide frame. I wasn't sure if he'd be in uniform or civilian clothes, so I just looked for his face instead of trying to spot uniforms as there were so many milling about.

A high pitched squeal directed my attention towards the toddler. Charlotte. She was running across the open space and jumping into the arms of a man in uniform.

A man who looked strikingly familiar.

A man who had the same midnight blue eyes as the little girl he was holding.

A man who I thought was my boyfriend...but was now embracing Charlotte's mother.

Ryan smiled down at the woman, and she smiled back at him, her arm around his waist and his around her shoulders. Charlotte was perched on his other arm, like she'd been there a thousand times before.

Because she probably had.

She was Ryan's daughter.

And the woman? Was she his *wife*?

What the hell was happening?

You want him to meet another girl? Someone who will fall in love with his big biceps and rock hard abs...someone who will get to see him look all sexy in his uniform? Then he'll fall in love with her, too. They'll get married and have babies, and you'll be nothing but a memory.

Ronnie's words from years ago haunted me, and I struggled to breathe, feeling like my life was flashing before my eyes. All the emails, the messages, the video chats, the phone calls...what were they?

Who was he?

He was a father. Possibly a husband.

I watched as the happy little family reunited before me.

What was I doing? Why was I still standing there?

I turned around, feeling nauseated, and picked up my Kindle, hastily stuffing it in the tote bag I'd packed to keep myself occupied while I waited for Ryan.

For my *boyfriend.*

Who I wanted to surprise with the great news that I was living in San Diego.

It looked like I was the one who was surprised in the end.

I took one last glance back, but they were already gone. My vision flooded with tears as I looked at the space where they'd once stood. Where he'd held his little girl and her beautiful mom.

Where he broke my heart.

~ **32** ~

Anna

I wasn't sure how I made it back to campus, but I did.

I wasn't sure how I made it to my dorm room, but I did.

I wasn't sure how I ended up in my bed, in my cozy pajamas, but I did.

I wasn't sure how I ended up with an awesome roommate, but I did.

I opened my swollen eyes later that evening to find Megan sitting across from me with two pints of Ben & Jerry's. I burst into tears.

"Oh, sweetie," Megan cooed, leaving her bed and lying beside me in mine. "What happened? I came home and you were in bed...alone...and I could tell you'd been crying."

I couldn't stop the tears. I wasn't supposed to be alone. I was supposed to be celebrating with Ryan. Ryan, the liar and cheater and...I didn't know what else, but it was bad.

How could he do that to me?

I wasted a year on him! It wasn't one-sided. It was very much two-sided. Maybe he didn't think he was a cheating asshole because he wasn't physically with me. Emotional cheating is still cheating.

"Anna? Talk to me," Megan begged, sounding desperate.

So I did. Between sobs, I told her everything. I unloaded years and years of love and pain and happiness and sadness. I let the tears fall as my roommate rubbed my back and whispered soothing words.

"Wow," Megan said when I was finished. "You've been through some stuff."

Unable to help myself, and quite possibly drunk on delirium, I laughed. I laughed and sobbed and laughed some more. Megan just had a way. She summed up the past five years of my life as "stuff." If only I could do the same.

"Want me to kick his ass? I could totally shank him."

"He's in the military, Meg," I managed to get the words out through sniffly giggles. "I doubt you could shank him."

"Of course, I could," she insisted. "He'd never expect it from me!"

She was right about that. She'd be the last person anyone would expect to be shanked by.

I inhaled a deep breath in, then let it out. Dr. Matson told me that controlling my breathing could help in times of stress and anxiety. It wasn't really working.

Ryan broke my heart.

Never, in a million years, would I have expected him to hurt me.

Was it revenge? Did I hurt him so badly all those years ago that he set off to break my heart like I did his? No, Ryan wasn't like that. Was he? I only knew the Ryan he portrayed...the Ryan in the airport, I didn't know him at all.

He had a daughter. A beautiful, adorable little girl with his eyes. A daughter he never once mentioned. Not even to my family because surely they wouldn't have kept it from me. *Charlotte.*

The waterworks began again and this time, Megan's humor couldn't stop them.

"Oh, Anna. It'll be okay, I promise. My high school boyfriend dumped me after graduation because he wanted to go away to college single. It sucks, sweetie, but it'll be okay."

But Ryan didn't dump me. He lied. He had a family. A fucking family!

"He said he loved me," I sobbed.

"He's an asshole."

I shook my head against my pillow. He wasn't an asshole.

But he was…wasn't he?

What kind of guy did that sort of thing? An asshole. That was who. We may not have done anything physically, but emotionally? We were all over each other emotionally.

I couldn't believe it. I couldn't believe this was the turn my life had taken.

"That's it," Megan said, rising from the bed. "We're going out!"

"What?"

"It's Saturday night. There's bound to be a party somewhere. We're going out. You need to get drunk!"

"I don't want to get drunk," I groaned, rolling towards the wall and pulling my blanket over my head. I wanted to stay in my warm little cocoon of darkness and self-pity.

"Too bad." She yanked the blanket off of me, and I whined in protest as the air conditioned air chilled my skin. I was in a pair of jersey knit sleep shorts and a matching tank top. My comfort clothes. She was ruining it.

"I really don't want to go out, Meg. Please let me wallow in peace."

"Nope, no wallowing." She pulled my arm until I was upright, and I reluctantly held myself up. "We're going to clean you up and make you look like the gorgeous woman you are, then we're going to go out and get you nice and drunk, and maybe even find you a hot guy to fool around with."

My eyes must have resembled a cartoon character, because I swore they popped right out of my head. "I'm not *fooling around* with anyone!"

She rolled her eyes. "Yeah, okay. Whatever. You won't fool around with anyone, but you're going to go out, get a little tipsy, and dance like nobody's looking. Got it?"

Her tone left no room for negotiation, and I growled as I stood from my bed and stomped off to our en suite bathroom. As I turned on the shower spray, I heard her cheers of delight and shook my head. She was something else. But I was glad I had her. With Megan around, I wouldn't be allowed to withdraw and feel sorry for myself. She'd make sure of it.

I'd only known her a little more than a month, but I had a feeling Megan and I would be very good friends.

***

"Chug! Chug! Chug! Chug!"

The crowd chanted as I downed my third beer bong of the night. Half of the cold, bitter liquid spilled down my face, but I didn't care. I was drunk. I was drunk before I even started the beer bongs. It was the shots that did me in.

I was kneeling on the disgusting kitchen floor of a house a bunch of seniors rented off campus. But I didn't care. My borrowed black mini skirt was so short that the entire room had caught a few shots of my red lace panties more than once—panties Megan insisted I wear since they matched the red lace bra I had on under my black tank top. I looked like a hooker, but I didn't care.

I didn't care about a damn thing.

It was wonderful.

I stood up after finishing the beer bong, raised my hands in the air in victory, and then swayed, leaning on some huge guy for support. He had a lot of muscles. Muscles on top of muscles. I wasn't scared of him though; he was like a teddy bear. He'd been following me around, growling at any guy who came close. *He was my bodyguard.* I laughed out loud at the thought.

I didn't even know his name.

"What's your name?" I asked him, at least I thought I did. The way he was looking at me indicated that I might not have made much sense. It sounded right in my head though.

I pointed to my chest and said, "Anna." Then I pointed to his chest.

"Jack," he said.

Oh good! He understood me. "Thank you, Jack," I said, patting him on the shoulder and moseying out of the kitchen. I headed for the living room, the last place I'd see Megan. She was dancing with some guy. I couldn't dance. The last time I danced was with Ryan at homecoming. That was over.

I spotted Megan in the corner, laughing with the guy she'd been dancing with earlier.

He was cute, but he was no Ryan. Ryan was beautiful. He was a beautiful jerk is what he was.

Someone bumped into me, and I almost fell down, but Jack caught me. I liked Jack. Why couldn't Ryan be more like Jack? Jack wouldn't have lied to me about having a daughter. He wouldn't emotionally cheat on me, either.

"Do you have a wife and daughter, Jack?"

His eyebrows furrowed. "No."

I beamed at my bodyguard. Everyone should be like Jack.

I leaned my head against Jack's chest, letting his strong body hold me up. "Thanks, Jack. I'll just be a minute."

He didn't respond. He didn't talk much. But that was okay because I was really, really tired. I closed my eyes, promising myself it would only be for a minute.

Just one minute...

~ **33** ~

Anna

Sunlight blasted through my bedroom window, and my eyeballs felt like they were about to explode. The university's drum line was parading around inside my skull, which didn't make any sense because Braddock didn't have a drum line. I wanted to take my head off and throw it out the window, right at that godforsaken sun!

Megan groaned from her bed, and I groaned back.

Then I sat straight up, immediately regretting the movement but too concerned to care.

How the hell did we get home?

"How did we get home?" I asked Megan.

"Too...loud," my wonderful roommate answered. My wonderful roommate who got me completely hammered last night. I rubbed my head...hammered...now I know where they got that term from because it felt like a tiny person was hammering inside my head. Maybe it was the seven dwarfs with their pickaxes.

"Megan, seriously. How did we get home?"

"Jack and John took us home." Her voice was muffled because she was talking to her pillow.

Jack and John? They sounded like a nursery rhyme. "Who are they?"

"Hot emo guy was John," she said, and I

vaguely recalled the guy she was dancing with. He could be considered a hot emo guy, I supposed. "Big bouncer looking dude was Jack." Ahh, Jack. I remembered him. He was my teddy bear bodyguard. "Pretty sure you fell asleep standing up, leaning on Jack. He came and got me and John, and we all piled in their car and they drove us home."

"Who were they?" I asked, gently laying back down on my bed.

"Seniors. They were friends of whoever's house that was. I think they're on the football team at San Diego State."

Made sense. Jack was huge, and SDSU wasn't too far away. Maybe it was their drum line in my head...

"Nothing happened, right?" I asked.

"No, nothing happened. They were perfect gentlemen. Jack carried you up here and then they took off."

I let out a relieved sigh, thankful I didn't make too many mistakes last night. I'd probably be feeling the liquid mistake for hours to come.

I picked up my phone from my nightstand—an annoying force of habit causing me to check my emails—but it was dead. I plugged it into the charger and powered it on, then rolled back over and pulled the covers over my head. There was nothing I needed from the outside world at that time. I only needed more sleep. Lots and lots more sleep.

"Jeez, Anna, get your damn phone," Megan grumbled. I peeled my eyes open. I must have fallen back asleep. The sun was still too bright, so I quickly snapped them shut.

I rolled over and blindly reached for my phone, holding it right in front of my face and squinting to see the screen. Seventeen missed calls and twenty-eight text messages.

What the hell?

Thinking there was a crisis—no one ever tried that hard to reach me—I unlocked the screen and tapped my way to my missed calls.

They were all from Ryan.

I tapped my message icon. Twenty-six of the messages were from Ryan, one was from Ronnie, and the last one was from an unknown number.

Well, I didn't really care what Ryan had to say, the jerk, so I opened the one from my sister.

Ronnie: Will you call Ryan back? He's blowing up my phone!

Ignoring that one. Once I told Ronnie why I wasn't speaking to Ryan, she would be Team Anna.

I opened the message from the unknown caller.

Unknown: This is Jack. Making sure you and Megan are all right.

Aw, how sweet. I knew he was a teddy bear. I texted him back.

Me: We're good, but very hungover. Thanks for getting us home last night.
Jack: Anytime. Just be careful if you go out and plan to drink that much. Not all guys

are as nice as my brother and me.

Brothers. Interesting.

"Did you know Jack and John were brothers?" I asked Megan.

"Maybe," she said, still talking to her pillow. "I don't know."

"Jack texted me. Wanted to make sure we're okay."

"That was nice of him."

"Yeah," I agreed.

Me: Duly noted. Thanks again, Jack.
Jack: You're welcome.

My finger-tip hovered over Ryan's message. Did I even want to know what he had to say? Not particularly. I decided to reply to Ronnie instead.

Me: Not speaking to Ryan.
Ronnie: What? Why?
Me: Long story. I'll call you later. Hung over.
Ronnie: You got drunk?!
Me: Yep. Feel like crap, too.
Ronnie: Serves you right.
Me: Thanks, sister.
Ronnie: That roommate is a bad influence on you.
Me: That roommate was a really great friend last night when I needed one. Cut her some slack. I'll explain later.
Ronnie: Whatever, I'm still better.
Me: Of course you're better, you're my sister. I need to go back to bed. Just ignore Ryan, okay?
Ronnie: Fine, but you better tell me what's

going on.
Me: I will. Love you, Ronnie.
Ronnie: Love you, too.

I looked at the time on my phone. 11:13. Still pretty early in hangover land. I could justify another hour of sleep. After turning the ringer off, I dropped the phone on my nightstand and closed my eyes.

***

After much deliberation, I chose not to tell Ronnie about what I saw at the airport. It was the first time I'd withheld something from my sister—aside from when I was in the bowels of depression following the shooting. My gut churned as I made up lie after lie, but for whatever reason, I didn't want to be the one to share that Ryan wasn't who we thought he was.

"We just got into a little fight, Ron. I don't feel like talking to him."

"You have been waiting to be with him for months, years if we're being honest, what could have possibly happened to make you not want to talk to him?"

"Nothing. It was just dumb stuff."

"If it was dumb, then I'm sure it'll all blow over," she said.

"Yeah, maybe," I hesitantly agreed, knowing damn well it would never just blow over. He lied to me. And his lie was nothing like my lie.

"I can't believe you actually got drunk last night," Ronnie said, and I could have hugged her through the phone for the subject change.

I laughed, the movement making me a little queasy. Maybe I wasn't completely out of the hangover zone. I laid back on my pillow and twisted a lock of hair around my finger.

"Megan and I went to a party. Who knew beer bongs could be so much fun?"

"Beer bongs?! Are you serious?"

"Not so loud," I whined.

"You have to be more careful than that, Anna."

"Yes, mom. Don't worry, I had a bodyguard," I told her, thinking of Jack

"Bodyguard?"

Shit.

"Yeah, the brother of Megan's friend," I answered. It wasn't a lie.

"So, a guy?" she inquired.

Double shit.

"Yes. His name is Jack. He's a really nice guy." I didn't know that for sure, but he didn't try anything last night, at least not that I remembered, so he had to be a good guy, right?

"What are you doing, Anna?"

I stiffened. I didn't have to defend myself. Not after what Ryan did. *But you didn't tell your sister what Ryan did,* my subconscious reminded me.

"I'm not doing anything. Nothing happened. He just stood by and warned off anyone who tried to approach me. Then he and his brother made sure Megan and I got home okay. I woke up this morning *alone* and fully clothed."

"I'm sorry, but don't get pissy with me. I just know you had a thing going with Ryan, and now all of a sudden he's back in San Diego—finally—and you're not speaking to him. *And* you're going to parties and drinking and hanging out with new guys--"

I cut her off. "I went to one party. I drank one time. I met two guys—who are just friends, mind you—at this one party. I'm not doing anything wrong, Ronnie. I'm a college student doing things a college student does."

I could practically feel her sigh through the line. "I know. I just worry about you."

I relaxed into the hard mattress. I knew my family would never stop worrying after what I put them through, and for that reason, I'd never ask them to.

"I know you do, Ron. But I'm okay. Really."

"Okay. But won't you at least talk to Ryan? If it's just something stupid, what's the big deal? You have so much history, are you ready to throw all that away?"

He already did.

"I'll think about it, okay?" Silence came across the line. "You still there?"

"Are you really not going to tell me what he did?" she asked quietly. "I know it's bigger than you're making it out to be."

I chewed my lip. I wanted to tell her, but I couldn't. Ronnie would support me completely, I knew that. She would be on her way to the airport with her pitchfork in a nanosecond. But I had to work through some of this stuff on my own before calling in reinforcements.

"I love you, Ronnie, you know that?"

She sighed again, undoubtedly frustrated with me. "Yeah. I do."

~ 34 ~

Ryan

Excited, confused, and annoyed. Those were the emotions I was alternating through as I stood on the Braddock campus, waiting for Anna to get out of class.

She was in San Diego and had been since August. She never told me, not once in all the times we'd talked over the last several months since she'd gotten her acceptance. Now I was in San Diego—she knew damn well when I was getting back—and she was ignoring me. Not a single phone call, text, or email.

Now I could see why.

She emerged from a brick building across the grassy field from where I stood, leaning against a tree. I was in the shade, so she wouldn't see me right away. Not that it would have mattered, since she was completely engrossed in whatever the giant steroid walking next to her was saying.

Then she laughed, the kind of laugh where her head tipped back, and she let it all out. The kind of laugh that made her entire body shake. The kind of laugh that meant she was familiar and comfortable with whomever she was with.

She was doing that laugh with *him*.

Who the fuck was he?

He smiled down at her, adoration in his eyes, like he was lost in the desert, and she was the last drink of water. And she grinned back at him. She wasn't supposed to be looking at other guys like that.

What the actual fuck was going on?

Didn't anything she said—anything we shared—mean a damn thing to her?

Walking down the gravel path through the field, they approached the tree I was still leaning against.

"Anna," I said coolly.

Her steps faltered and Steroid grasped her arm to steady her. I glared at where he was touching her with such a gentle familiarity.

"Ryan," she gasped, surprise evident on her face.

I laughed, but nothing about the situation was funny. "You seem surprised to see me, which is interesting considering *you* know *I* live here."

"How...how did you..." she trailed off.

I stood up to my full height and stepped away from the tree, pleased I was both taller and wider than the goon still standing beside her.

"Well, when my *girlfriend* didn't respond to my phone calls, texts, and emails, I called her sister because I was worried. Imagine my surprise when her sister told me she was here, in San Diego. Ronnie was even more surprised that you and I hadn't seen each other yet, considering the disagreement we'd apparently gotten into."

She had the nerve to look down at the ground, as if this was awkward and painful for *her*.

"Can we talk about this in private?" she asked, and I let out another laugh. Again, nothing funny about this.

"Why? So your new boyfriend doesn't find out about how you've been playing him?"

"Hey, take it easy, guy," Steroid said, taking a step between us.

"Why don't you just fuck off?" I asked, getting in his face.

"Stop it!" Anna shouted, moving between us and pushing us apart, one hand on each of our chests. Her touch burned me, but not as badly as seeing her hand on someone else burned.

"You know, that's real rich coming from you," she said, her sharp gaze like a knife in my chest.

"What are you talking about? What the hell have I done? You're the one who is with someone else." I'd be damned if she turned this on me.

Steroid smirked. He fucking smirked.

"Jack is my friend. He has a girlfriend, Cindy, who is right over there," Anna said, pointing to a short brunette sitting on a blanket in the grass, amused at the spectacle unfolding before her. "I'm not with *anyone*. Not even you." *What the fuck?* She turned to Steroid, or Jack. "I'm sorry, I'm not feeling up for lunch. Apologize to Cindy for me."

He nodded and gave her arm a friendly squeeze—too damn friendly, if you asked me, which no one did—and then he turned to me and glared. "You hurt her any more than you already have, I'll kick your fucking ass. I don't give a shit who you are." Then he stormed off, joining his petite girlfriend for a picnic.

Anna took one long look at me, and all I saw was sadness in her glassy eyes. Taking a closer look, I noticed things I hadn't seen in my previous rage. The way her skin looked a little too pale and the corners of her mouth were downcast. It reminded me of when...

"What's going on?" I asked, unease spreading through my body. She just shook her head at me and turned away, but not before I saw a tear slip down her cheek. "Anna, wait," I said, grabbing her arm gently. "Talk to me," I urged.

She turned back around and my heart ached—it actually ached—at the sight of her flooded eyes and wet face.

"Baby, what's wrong?" I asked, holding her other arm, too. I was too afraid that if I let go, she'd disappear again.

She pulled herself away from me and sniffed. She looked...broken.

"I saw you," she whispered, as though it was too painful to say out loud.

"Saw me what?" What was she talking about?

She met my eyes again and the pain I saw in them was raw. Selfishly, I thought that this was worse than how she was after the shooting because this time the pain was aimed at me. At something I had done. But what?

"At the airport."

The airport? Shit. Charlotte. And Kelsey. Shit shit shit.

"It's not what you think," I told her, which was a lie because it was at least half of what she thought.

"Just save it, Ryan," she said, sounding utterly defeated.

It was my fault she looked and sounded the way she did, and I hated it. If I'd just been honest with her from the start, I could have avoided causing her pain.

"No, just hear me out."

"I don't want to hear you out," she snapped. "Was this all just a scheme for revenge?" she asked, clenching her fists by her sides.

"What? No!"

"Look, I get it. I hurt you when I pushed you away--"

"No, you don't get it," I interrupted. "It has nothing to do with revenge. I didn't say anything about Charlotte because I wasn't sure how to bring it up. When we started talking again, you were so...fragile." She rolled her eyes at that, but at least she wasn't running away. Not yet. "And then when things...evolved...I was never sure of the right time."

"How about any time? Any time would have been the right time, Ryan. I'm so sick of everyone treating me with kid gloves. I get it, all right? I was lost for a while, and everyone felt they needed to walk on eggshells around me. They still do. But dammit, I'm not going to break!"

"I'm sorry, Anna."

"Sorry for what? Sorry for leading me on? For not telling me you have a daughter...a family?" her voice broke on the last word.

"Hold on, you're misunderstanding. I'm not with Charlotte's mom. We're just friends."

"Yeah. Right. Well, I have to go," she said, sniffling again.

"Please, can we talk about this?" I threaded my hands behind my head, the only thing I could do to keep myself from reaching for her.

"I don't think so," she said, shaking her head.

"Anna," I begged. I didn't know what else to say. I screwed up. Kelsey warned me. She fucking warned me this would happen.

"Bye, Ryan."

I stood there like an idiot, watching the love of my life walk away from me, feeling like my heart was being torn out of my chest and dragged behind her for the second time.

Only this time, it was my fault.

~ 35 ~

Anna

Returning to my room, I was thankful Megan had a class. I wanted to wallow alone. He looked so beautiful...so handsome...so angry. As if he had the right to be any of those things. He was a liar.

Lying down on my bed, I stared at the white popcorn ceiling, wondering if those tiny little points were sharp to the touch. Every time I looked at the ceiling of my dorm room, I wanted to take one of those electric sanders to it and make it smooth. I couldn't understand the appeal of a ceiling with tiny little peaks and ridges.

My phone pinged, and I knew it was Ryan. I could feel it.

I wanted to believe him about Charlotte. I wanted to believe he was waiting for the right moment before time slipped away. I wanted to, but that was such a convenient response. A clichéd response.

The phone pinged again, and I sighed, rolling over to pull it from my backpack.

Ryan: I'm so sorry, Anna. I was going to tell you as soon as I got back. I meant what I said. I didn't want to tell you in the beginning because I was afraid of your response. I didn't want to upset you. You were doing so well, becoming you again. I didn't want to ruin that. I didn't think it would be a big deal because we were just friends. When we started talking, I had no idea I'd fall in love with you all over again. Then I wanted to tell you, but I wanted to wait until I got home so we could talk about it in person. You were right, though. I should have told you in the beginning. I shouldn't have kept her from you. I'm not ashamed of her, only of myself, because Charlotte's the most amazing little girl in the world and I shouldn't have hidden her from you, or from your family. I was wrong and I'm sorry.

Another came through.

Ryan: Charlotte's mom's name is Kelsey. We're not together. We had a one night stand a few years ago that resulted in Charlotte. When she told me she was pregnant, we agreed we'd do the whole thing together. We tried to date, but it just wasn't happening. We've been friends, good friends, ever since. That's all. Kelsey knows about you. She told me months ago that I should have told you about Charlotte. I should have listened. I should have had faith in your strength and in our friendship, and I should have been honest from the beginning. I'm sorry, Anna. Please forgive me.

Staring down at the screen of my phone, I pondered what to do. On the one hand, I wanted to forgive him. I wanted everything to go back to the way it was a week ago when I was sitting at the airport, excitedly waiting for his plane to arrive. On the other hand, I worried that maybe we just rushed into the whole thing and didn't really know each other as well as we'd thought. Case in point, he had a whole life I knew nothing about. A daughter I knew nothing about.

Things moved so quickly between us, they always had. Returning my attention to my phone, I typed out a response.

Me: I don't really know what to do here, Ryan. I need some time. Please give me that.

His response was almost instant.

Ryan: I'll give you time, just don't give up on me. Please.

I didn't respond. I couldn't. I wouldn't give him any false hope or empty promises. I also didn't want to hurt him and I knew rushed responses often led to saying things you didn't mean. I couldn't think of a single response that wouldn't do one of the above, so I said nothing.

***

"It sounds like you feel he let you down," Dr. Matson said, her face reflecting understanding. I'd just finished telling her all about my run-in on campus with Ryan.

"He did let me down. He has a daughter! A daughter. That's a huge piece of his life he should have shared, don't you think? I mean, we talked about everything...shared everything...and he left that part out."

"How do you feel about him having a

daughter?"

Running a hand through my hair, I thought about her question. How did I feel?

"I'm not upset about Charlotte, and I'm not jealous that he was with someone else. We were separated for years. It wasn't like I'd hoped he spent all that time pining over me. Neither of us could have ever imagined we'd reconnect."

Dr. Matson nodded as I spoke. "You're just upset he wasn't forthcoming."

"Yeah...when I thought about our future, I didn't imagine having to take a kid into consideration. I'm not even talking about long-term stuff here. Ryan being a dad will affect us going on dates, spending the night together...there's a whole other person to factor into all sorts of decisions—big and small."

"So Ryan having a daughter has put a kink in your plans?"

"It sounds so selfish when you put it that way, but yes. I don't have any negative feelings towards her. She seemed like a sweetheart when I met her at the airport. I'm sure she's a good kid, and she's part of Ryan so I have no doubt I could love her, but I'm just not sure I'm in a place in my life where it would be wise to bring a child into the picture."

"What do you mean by that?"

I studied my keyboard as I answered. "I'm crazy, right? Who wants their kid around a crazy person?"

"Anna, you're not crazy. You're far from it. You experienced a trauma, you had an emotional reaction to that trauma, and you're working on getting past it. That doesn't sound like a crazy person to me—which, by the way, is not an appropriate psychological term—it sounds like a strong person, a person who knows what she wants and is working to achieve it."

"I *am* trying to achieve it," I said quietly, still looking at the QWERTY line of the keyboard.

"You still can—you *are*. Anna, haven't you noticed all the positive changes you've made in your life? You are very different from the girl who returned home last December. You've achieved the goals you set for yourself. You're in college now and you're thriving outside of your comfort zone. You're doing well in your classes...what about that makes you think you're crazy?"

"None of it, I guess. But this is a big thing, Dr. Matson. It's not like he forgot to tell me he was a part-time stripper. He has a child."

"It is a big thing. You did say he planned on telling you, right?"

"He said he wanted to tell me in person so we could talk about it," I answered.

"But you two haven't talked about it yet, not really."

"No. I didn't want to talk to him when I saw him, so he texted me."

"From what you told me about his messages, they didn't really address your main concerns."

"No. I mean, I feel better because I know he wasn't cheating on me—or her."

"But you're still unsure about how you want to move forward with him."

"Yes."

"Whenever we've talked about Ryan, you always mention your history. You're comfortable with him because he's familiar. You love him because he listens to you, and you feel as though he genuinely cares about you. He makes you laugh, and he takes care of you in a way that doesn't feel patronizing. Have any of those things changed since you found out about Charlotte?"

"Not really, no. All the history and the feelings are still there."

"So it's just the future that has changed."

"Yes," I responded, not sure where she was going with this.

"Have you and Ryan talked about the future?"

"Nothing major, I guess. Just how we couldn't wait to see each other, and that we'd see each other while he was on leave. We may have said some other vague things about doing stuff together in the future."

"So he did see a future with you?"

"Yes."

"And he didn't seem concerned about you being in Charlotte's life? Surely, he was thinking about it; he's her dad. If he's so good at taking care of you, he's probably good at taking care of her, too, don't you think?"

"I guess so," I said, noncommittally.

"You have a lot to think about here, Anna. I don't think you should make a rash decision. Seriously consider your options, okay?" She waited for me to nod before continuing. "What's your next move?"

"I guess we should talk."

"Communication is extremely important in any relationship, as you both now know."

I refrained from rolling my eyes, and instead smiled and thanked Dr. Matson for the impromptu video session.

Picking up my cell phone, I typed out a quick text to Ryan before I chickened out.

Me: Let's talk.

~ **36** ~

Anna

I was all nerves as I waited on a bench in a small park just off campus. I bounced my foot, watching children play in a nearby playground and wondering if Ryan ever took Charlotte to the park. Of course he did. Ryan was probably Superdad, with a big red S on his spandex-covered chest.

"Hey," his voice came out of nowhere, and I startled. "Sorry." He stood beside the bench with his hands in the pockets of his jeans, and his shirt stretched tightly against his chest. He was hot, even in a plain white t-shirt.

"Hi." I scooted over on the bench so he could sit.

"Thanks." He took the seat beside me, rested his elbows on his knees and gazed over to the playground.

"Do you have one of those near your place for Charlotte?" I asked, hoping to let him know I was open to talking about her.

A small smile graced his face. "Yeah. There's a small jungle gym in our apartment complex, and there's a park nearby, too."

"Do you and Kelsey live together?" I asked. He'd said "our apartment complex," and I had to know what he meant.

"No. I live with Rogers. Kelsey and Charlotte have an apartment in the same building. We work it out that way so we're always close."

"She moves with you?" I wasn't sure I wanted to hear the answer to that question. I understood the concept of knowledge being power, but I was beginning to get a sense of just how close his relationship—friendship— with Kelsey was, and it was making me uneasy.

"Yeah. She works from home doing web design so she can pretty much work from anywhere. We agreed early on that as long as she could, she'd live wherever the Navy took me so Charlotte would grow up with her dad in her life. If she didn't...well, who knows when I'd see her with deployments and relocations? I couldn't just see my kid on leave, you know? She'd never remember me. Kelsey has sacrificed a lot for me, living the life of a military wife without many of the benefits."

"Why aren't there benefits?"

He gave me a weird look but answered anyway. "We're not married, so she doesn't really have access to the support network military spouses do. She has to pay for her own insurance—Charlotte's on mine. Other stuff like that."

Those weren't the kinds of benefits I'd been thinking about, and he knew it. Now I understood the weird look he'd given me.

"There's really nothing between you two?"

"No. There's absolutely nothing between us. We're just friends. Good friends. We have to be to raise Charlotte the way we've been." He took a deep breath and blew it out, still looking out at the playground. "I'm sorry I kept it from you."

"I know." I believed him, I did. It was easy to see he was sorry by the way his usually commanding posture was sunken. "I'm sorry I avoided you when I found out, I just...I didn't know how to process what I'd seen."

We were silent for a few long moments before he spoke. "So...are you not ignoring me now?"

I glanced over at him just as he peeked at me, and I giggled. It felt like ninth grade art class all over again, butterflies and all.

"I'm not ignoring you anymore."

He leaned back against the bench and reached for my hand. "Good, because I missed you."

"I missed you, too." Yep, butterflies.

It was easy to confess that. It was *Ryan*, after all. He was *the* guy. *My* guy. Was he the same guy I thought I knew, though? I glanced at his face, then down to where our hands were still intertwined. He still looked the same, sounded the same, felt the same...but he *was* different. He had a daughter. *He was a dad.* I didn't begrudge him that, not now that I knew the truth and knew he hadn't been cheating, but was this something I wanted to be part of? I still didn't know.

Anger brewed inside me, once again, as I thought about him taking that choice away from me. For ruining what had developed between us.

"You're still upset," he observed.

Damn right I was.

Communication is extremely important in any relationship. Dr. Matson's words repeated in my head.

"You let me fall in love with you without

informing me you were—are—a package deal. I have my own set of issues, what right do I have to bring those into the life of a child? By not telling me, you didn't let me decide if this was something I want for myself...for my life."

"Anna, I'm not asking you to be a mother to Charlotte."

I snatched my hand away from him and stood from the bench, clenching my fists by my sides before I turned to him. "I know that. My point is, you took away my choice, Ryan. Part of my therapy has been taking charge of my own life and making my own decisions...owning them. You took that away from me. I called you my boyfriend, thinking the most complicated part of planning our dates would be picking what restaurant to eat at, not wondering if it was your time with Charlotte or if you could get a babysitter. It's not a big deal to me that you have a daughter, Ryan. What's a big deal is that you brought me into your life without telling me about something—someone—big enough to make an impact on our relationship. You blindsided me."

"I know, and I'm sorry. I should have told you from the beginning. I know that. I was wrong. Nothing has to change--"

"Are you nuts? Everything has changed!" I yelled at him.

He was standing now, too, his hands raised in a "calm down" gesture. People in the park were looking at us, but I didn't care.

"I'm still the same guy, Anna. I'm still the guy you met in art class. The guy who held your hair back while you threw up after Sandy Martin's party your sophomore year.

Who you laid with under the stars countless nights and who you planned your future with."

I shook my head. "But you're not that same guy, Ryan. Not really. You're a dad, and that will always come first. And that's okay; it's the way it should be. I'm just not sure I fit in your world right now."

His eyes searched mine desperately. "Of course you do. I know all about your—as you put it—*issues*, and I don't think they're as big a problem as you're making them out to be. I've seen you grow as a person since you came back, and I'm not worried. You're a good person with a huge heart. If that's your main concern, we can work through it."

"I don't know that we can. I'm sorry, Ryan, but I don't think I can do this, not right now."

"What are you saying? You need more time to think?"

"I'm saying..." My heart broke as I thought the words. But I wasn't ready to do this, not really. Like with everything else involving Ryan, I jumped right in. I still needed time to think, to process. And it wasn't fair to just drag him along while I did that. "I think I need to focus more on me right now."

His shoulders slumped as defeat spread across his face. "And what does that mean for us?"

"There is no us."

~ **37** ~

Ryan

There is no us.

Her words haunted me hours after our confrontation in the park.

She was right about everything. In hindsight, I realized that. I never took into consideration the fact that I hadn't let Anna decide whether she wanted to be in a relationship with a father. I'd treated my own daughter like an accessory and not a person. Of course she was a big deal—the biggest—and I minimized her existence.

I was a shit.

Ignoring the knock on my apartment door, I took another pull from my beer. I wasn't in the mood to talk to anyone.

There is no us.

I heard a key enter and turn the lock and groaned. Kelsey. She was the only one beside Rogers who had a key, and he wouldn't have knocked first. I wasn't in the mood for her "I told you so" bullshit. In the years we'd been raising Charlotte, Kelsey and I never fought, but if she walked in and mouthed off about Anna, it would happen now.

"You haven't answered your phone," she said once inside. She was alone because Charlotte was in daycare until 4:00 so Kelsey could work from home and actually get things done.

"I don't want to talk."

She cocked her head to the side. "What's wrong?"

"Nothing." Everything.

"Ryan," she said, using her mom tone on me. Wouldn't work. "Is this about Anna? Did you finally talk to her?"

Kelsey knew I hadn't been able to get in touch with Anna, but she didn't know why. She didn't know Anna had seen us at the airport and thought we were a family. She didn't know about our...fight...whatever it was. She didn't know that we were over.

"Ry, what's this about? You're acting broody and drinking beer at 2:00 in the afternoon. What's going on?"

"If I tell you, you better not say you told me so," I warned her.

She nodded understandingly and took a seat on the couch beside me, tucking her legs underneath her. "Tell me," she said.

So I did. Everything from the airport to the campus to the park. I told her how she'd been right all along, and I admitted that I should have listened to her and told Anna about Charlotte a long time ago.

"Wow...so she's here," she said, and it wasn't a question.

"She is, and she's pissed and hurt and I don't know what to do about it."

"She has the right to be upset, Ryan."

"I know that. I admitted I was wrong, okay?"

"Don't get testy with me because you dug yourself a hole so deep you can't get out of it."

Fuck.

"Sorry, Kels."

"It's not me you should be apologizing to."

"I already apologized to Anna, and she won't accept. She's not even pissed at me for hiding Charlotte. She's pissed at me for taking away her choice."

Kelsey was silent for a full minute before she spoke. "Well, it sounds like she needs to be in control, or at least feel like she's in control, and you took that away from her. You need to find a way to give that control back."

"I don't know how to do that," I said, running my hand through my short hair.

"Me either. But you're probably going to need to take a few steps back. You guys were near the finish line together, but now she's back at the starting line and you're still at the end. You need to move yourself back to where she is. This is a whole new ball game for her. Nothing has changed for you, but everything has changed for her."

Damn it. She was absolutely right. Of course it wouldn't be easy for Anna to simply move forward after having a three year old bomb dropped on her.

"Is it selfish of me to say I don't want to move backwards? I want to keep moving forward?"

Kelsey sighed, resting back into the cushions of the couch. "It is selfish, but it makes sense for you to feel that way. You just have to have patience, Ry."

Patience. Right. Not my strong suit. Not after spending years apart and finally being back in a comfortable place with Anna.

"Patience," Kelsey repeated.

I laid my head back on the couch and closed my eyes.

Now, I waited.

***

Kelsey left a few minutes later, after I assured her I wasn't going to have anything else to drink so she could drop Charlotte off with me after daycare. She had to finish a big project for work, and wouldn't be able to do it with Charlotte under foot.

I hadn't even drunk half of my beer, so I poured it down the drain and cleaned up around the apartment while I waited for my daughter. Rogers was a pig, but he was my best friend and otherwise an easy roommate, so I let it pass.

At 4:15 on the dot, the apartment door burst open, and my little ray of sunshine burst in.

"Daddy!" she squealed, jumping into my arms. It never got old. I could see her every day for a week, and she was always this excited.

"Hey, princess. How was your day?"

As I listened to Charlotte tell me everything about the finger-painting they did today, I waved goodbye to Kelsey as she snuck out the door. As excited as Charlotte was to see me, she still didn't like for her mother to leave her.

"Can I see your pictures?"

Charlotte frowned. "Have to dwy, Daddy. Tomowwow."

I smiled at her serious little face. "Tomorrow sounds perfect."

I followed her around as she investigated the space. It was the exact same layout as Kelsey's apartment, where Charlotte lived full-time, but the décor was different, and it amused my daughter to no end. I've been going to their apartment because, until yesterday, most of mine and Rogers' things were still in boxes.

"This is the wady fwom the aiwpowt."

Charlotte was standing in front of my nightstand, looking at a picture of me and Anna from high school. It was a selfie she'd taken while we were at the lake. Both our faces were pink from the sun, and we were laughing at something. I couldn't remember what. We were always laughing back then, before everything got...complicated.

"That's my friend, Anna. You saw her?"

"Her was weally nice."

My pulse quickened. "You talked to her?"

Charlotte nodded, the movement exaggerated. "Wight befowe you came. Her is pwetty."

"Yeah, princess, she is pretty."

"Did she want to see you at the aiwpowt, too?"

"I think she did, baby girl."

"Can she come over and pway wif me?"

I rubbed my chest. I wanted Anna to come over and play with Charlotte. More than anything. But that was just me being selfish again.

"Maybe someday, princess."

I hoped that was true.

~ **38** ~

Anna

A sense of déjà vu rolled through me as I made my way across campus exactly two weeks after my first confrontation with Ryan. Everything felt the same, sans Jack, who had to meet Cindy at the student center after class.

As I walked by the tree where Ryan had been waiting, a woman stepped out from behind the thick trunk. "Anna?" she asked.

She stepped out of the shadows, and I recognized her immediately. Kelsey. I held back my groan and plastered on a fake smile.

"Can I help you?"

"Do you have a minute to talk?" She must have known I recognized her from the airport because she didn't introduce herself, which meant Ryan must have told her everything.

Great.

I nodded, not wanting to make an enemy of Ryan's baby mama in case he and I ended up friends again in the future. I didn't want there to be any friction between us.

She followed behind me as I led her over to a bench down the gravel path and sat beside me once we stopped.

"I'm sorry for blindsiding you like this, but I wanted to talk to you about Ryan...and Charlotte."

"Okay," I hoped she'd just get this over with. Maybe she was there to tell me to back off, that *she* was in love with Ryan. Maybe she didn't want me around her kid; I couldn't exactly blame her. Who knew what Ryan had shared about me and our past? I never expected what she did say.

"Look, Ryan's a great guy. I know you know that already, though. He and I have been close the last four years, but you and him...you go way back. You probably know a lot more about him than I do, and I won't pretend that you don't. He made a mistake. A big, stupid mistake. I told him months ago that he should have been upfront with you about Charlotte. He thought he knew what he was doing. He's an idiot, but he's still a great guy. I'm not asking you to do anything you're not comfortable with...I get why you broke things off...but don't write him off completely. Not yet." She broke eye contact and her eyes scanned the field. She lightly shook her head, as if trying to clear it.

"Kelsey, I appreciate you coming out here and talking to me. You're right, I do know Ryan's a great guy. I'm just not sure our lives are heading down the same path anymore." It hurt to say the words, but they were true. I wasn't sure we were headed in the same direction. Things were different from when we were a couple of teenagers planning our future. I'd been stupid to think they hadn't been. Things changed. *People* changed.

"He's been so lost the past two weeks," she said, still staring off in the distance. "Since he's been home, really. You're a part of him. Such a big part. I knew that all along; we're very open with each other." She sighed, and I was beginning to think she was about to drop the "stay away from my man" line, but again, she surprised me.

"Ryan would kill me for saying this. Hell, he'd kill me for coming here. We never fight, I don't know if he ever told you that, but we don't. We've never had a reason to. One night while he was on the ship, we were talking after his video chat with Charlotte, and he was talking about you and how he'd eventually want you to meet Charlotte. I figured that day would come eventually since you two were getting close again. I knew it was inevitable. I mean, if not you, someone, you know? Either he or I would eventually meet someone we'd want to introduce to her. He was talking about you meeting Charlotte, and he was so excited and do you know what I told him?"

I shook my head because I had absolutely no idea. It was the weirdest conversation, mostly one-sided, I'd had in a long time.

"I told him I was reluctant for you to meet her because of your history. I was scared that you might not be stable enough to be around our daughter." A tear ran down her cheek. "He got so mad at me. He had such faith in you, in his judgement as a father, that he was positive nothing would ever happen that would bring your character into question around Charlotte. I argued with him, and he argued back, and we didn't speak for a while after that, only cordial greetings and the necessary updates about Charlotte." She wiped her cheek and rubbed her hands on her jeans. "He told me that was one of the concerns you had when you two argued. I wanted you to know, as a third party who had the same thought herself, I'm not worried about you being around Charlotte. Not anymore. I trust in Ryan's faith in you."

"I don't know what to say."

"You don't have to say anything, Anna. I saw you with Charlotte at the airport. I know it was only a minute, and I didn't know it was you at the time, but you were good with her. And Ryan trusts you, that's enough for me. Just...have a little faith in yourself. And in Ryan. He'd never ask you to walk through his life with him and expect you to do it alone. That's what you do in relationships. You and your partner walk through everything together. That's what he and I do as Charlotte's parents. We make choices together and carry each other when one of us is too weak. It's what I do when he's deployed and what he does when he gets back. It's a give and take, always a give and take. Let him give, Anna. He wants to."

"You make it sound so easy," I said, leaning against the back of the bench.

"Who says it can't be easy?"

"Are three-year-olds ever easy?"

She laughed, a beautiful, melodic sound. "No, no, they're not. They're work. A lot of work. But it's worth it. The smiles, macaroni art, hugs, and sloppy kisses are totally worth it. I know it's a big decision. A relationship with Ryan means a relationship with Charlotte. A relationship with Charlotte means a relationship with me. He comes with a lot of baggage, I get that. It's scary and intimidating. It was scary and intimidating when I found out I was pregnant, too, by a guy in the Navy who was five years my junior.

But it's worth it. I promise you, we're all worth it."

When I didn't answer her, she said one more thing. "Are you really ready to say goodbye to him for good? It seems to me, the two of you are meant to be together. Don't let him go, Anna."

With one last smile, she stood from the bench and walked off.

Could I let him go?

~ **39** ~

Anna

Before I chickened out, I wrapped my knuckles three times on the apartment door.

It wasn't easy getting Ryan's address, but after I finally told Ronnie everything, she agreed to help me. I didn't know what she said or did to get it, but less than an hour after I'd hung up the phone with her, she texted me his address.

I waited a full minute, then knocked again. No answer. Wouldn't that just be the case? I finally made a decision, and he wasn't home.

Sitting on the top step of the third floor landing, I rested my head in my hands.

Two days after my run-in with Kelsey, and I'd decided. I didn't want to let him go.

Was I scared? Yes.

Did I have any idea what I was getting myself into? Not really.

But one thing was for certain. I was madly in love with Ryan Jacobs, and I wasn't letting him go. Kelsey had been right. Whatever happened...it would be worth it, and I wouldn't have to face it alone. I'd have Ryan and...oddly enough, I knew I'd have Kelsey, too.

"You okay?" a voice asked, startling me.

Lifting my head, I was met with the brown eyes of a man about Ryan's height and build, maybe a little taller, with a friendly smile on his face. He was also wearing a blue, multicolored patterned uniform. The patch over his left breast pocket read "US Navy." My eyes brightened.

"I'm looking for Ryan. Ryan Jacobs. Do you know him? He's in 306."

The guy's smile grew wider. "Yeah, he's my roommate. Are you...are you Anna?"

I nodded and looked at the patch on his right breast pocket. "And you're Rogers."

"Yeah, but my first name is Keith."

Standing, I extended my hand. "It's nice to meet you."

"Same here," he said, and I immediately liked his easygoing personality. "Want to wait inside? We just got off duty, but he was stopping by the store on his way back."

"Thank you," I told him, following him to the door.

He ushered me inside and motioned to the couch. "I'm going to go shower but have a seat. He shouldn't be more than five minutes behind me."

"Thanks," I said, taking a seat on the brown leather sofa. When Keith headed for his bedroom, I looked around the space. It was a bachelor pad, for sure, with a brown leather couch and recliner and dark wood furniture in the living room. There was a pink plastic tub in the corner of the room, below the large flat screen TV that was mounted to the wall; that probably held Charlotte's toys. The kitchen was small, containing only a small four-seater table and chairs. The walls of both rooms were bare.

I was about to get up and investigate the toy chest when the front door opened, and there he stood.

He was frozen in place, staring at me on his couch...in his apartment...like if he did so much as blink, I'd disappear.

"Hi," I said lamely.

"Hey," he said, equally as lame.

I'd practiced an entire speech on the Uber ride over, but my mind went completely blank at the sight of him.

"You're here," he let the door close behind him finally.

"I'm here," I said with a small rise and fall of my shoulders.

He took a few steps towards me and I stood, meeting him in the middle of the room. He raised his hand, then dropped it just as fast.

"Ryan," I started to say just as he said, "I'm sorry."

We both laughed. It was awkward. We were never awkward.

Lifting his hand again, he cupped the side of my face. I leaned into his touch and closed my eyes. "It's so good to see you."

"It's good to see you, too," I said softly. He went to move his hand, but I brought mine up to hold it in place. "Don't let me go, Ryan." Opening my eyes, I looked into his deep blues and repeated myself. "Don't let me go."

"Never, baby. Never."

He leaned in, and his lips brushed against mine. It had been years since I felt his soft kiss, but it seemed like only yesterday. It was so familiar, so...him. I returned the kiss, snaking my arms around his waist. He wrapped his arms around me and pulled me closer.

A throat cleared behind us, and I jumped,

breaking our connection.

I rested my cheek on Ryan's chest as he glared at Keith over my shoulder. "Can I help you?"

"Just wondering if you wanted me to order the pizza?" Rogers asked.

Ryan cursed under his breath and grabbed my hand, pulling me past a grinning Keith and down the small hallway. "Order whatever you want," he called out before pulling me into his bedroom and slamming the door shut.

I almost melted under the heat from his gaze as he turned around and looked at me. Wasting no time, he pressed me up against the bedroom door and kissed me again.

"I missed you so much," he said in between kisses.

"I missed you, too," I told him. "We should talk," I added when he let me come up for air.

"Talk. Right." He pressed one more kiss against my lips and reluctantly stepped away.

Giving myself a moment to take him in, I almost whimpered at how he looked in his uniform. I'd seen him from the shoulders up through the video chat, but I hadn't gotten the full effect. He must have been melting panties all around the world. He made my heart flutter and my knees go week; it was a good thing I was sitting down.

"See something you like?" he asked, using the words he'd first said to me when he caught me eyeing him in art class.

Smirking, I replied just as I had that day. "Nothing much."

"Liar," he said, stalking back towards me.

Giggling, I pushed my hands against his

chest. "Talk. Remember?"

He groaned in response and took a seat on his bed, patting the space beside him. I sat, noticing the picture of us from a summer at the lake on his nightstand. It warmed my heart to see that even though things weren't quite right between us, he still kept me close.

"Tell me you have good news," he said, a solemn look on his face.

I wanted to reassure him, but I couldn't...not entirely. I couldn't make empty promises about our future because anything could happen. He and I both knew that more than anybody. So I told him the truth. I told him what I knew at that moment.

"I want to be part of your life, Ryan. I want to try. I have no idea what I'm getting myself into, but I love you, and I don't want to lose you."

He closed his eyes and dropped his head, the tension that had been holding him together so stiffly seeming to disappear from his body in one giant rush.

Opening his eyes again, he placed his hands on my cheeks. "You have no idea how happy I am to hear you say that." He gave me a quick kiss, then pulled away. "I'm so sorry, Anna. What I did was shitty, but I swear, I'm going to spend the rest of my life making it up to you, if you'll let me."

"I want to let you," I whispered against his lips.

"Thank God," he said, closing the distance between us.

We never did make it back out to the living room for pizza, but it was worth it.

~ Epilogue ~

Ryan

Five Years Later

"I'm so proud of you," I told my wife as I looked around the wide, open space.

"I couldn't have done it without you," Anna said, her eyes glittering in the bright, white lights.

"No, babe. This is all you."

We were at her first showing, and the pieces she'd worked tirelessly on over the years were displayed on the walls of one of Seattle's finest art galleries. Black and white sketches and colorful abstract paintings were strategically placed throughout the room.

The click of heels on the hardwood floor alerted us to our first visitor, and we turned, hand-in-hand, to greet them.

"This is amazing," Kelsey cried, hugging Anna first, then me.

"Great work," Jim, Kelsey's husband, added. We shook hands, and he kissed Anna on the cheek.

Anna looked behind them, frowning. "Charlotte didn't come?"

Kelsey laughed. "And leave her baby brother behind with the sitter? Come on, no one can take care of Brody as well as his big sister."

Brody was our four month old son—mine and Anna's—and he was spending the evening with Kelsey and Jim's two kids and their babysitter...and Charlotte, too, apparently.

Anna's eyes filled with love. She and Charlotte were close. When properly introduced five years ago, they took to each other immediately and formed a bond Kelsey and I couldn't touch.

"She's such a little mommy," Anna agreed, probably remembering, like me, how Charlotte wouldn't let Kelsey and Jim's twins out of her sight their first six months.

"The party can officially start. I'm here." We all laughed as Ronnie rolled into the room, her fiancé, Dave, walking beside her.

Anna bent down to hug her sister, then greeted Dave.

I looked at my watch. "Doors don't open to the public for another twenty minutes."

"There's already a line outside," Dave told us, and Anna's face paled.

"A line?"

"You're a big deal," I joked. I'd been telling her that ever since she started winning awards for her art back in college. She just rolled her eyes as she always did.

"The 'rents should be here soon. They're just parking the car."

It warmed my heart that our friends and family traveled from all over to support Anna. Her parents, my parents, and Ronnie all still lived on the east coast in North Carolina. They'd wanted to be closer to us and to Brody and Charlotte, but considering I moved every few years with the Navy, it didn't make sense for them to attempt to settle near us until I retired. Rogers ended up heading back to Norfolk after San Diego—the first time he and I had been separated during our service—but he'd be here tonight, too, with his girlfriend. And Anna's old college roommate, Megan, was in town as well. Kelsey and Jim were local, Kelsey having moved to Seattle with Anna and me when I had my last relocation. She met Jim here, and they lived in a house in the same neighborhood as me and Anna. I had a feeling this was the last stop for Kelsey, though. But I didn't want to think about that tonight, tonight was about my wife and her art.

"This is all so wonderful," Anna's mom said as she walked through the room towards us. Her eyes were wide as she took everything in. "I've seen your work, darling, but I've never seen it all in one place like this." She kissed Anna on both cheeks, then smiled at her. "I'm so proud of you."

"Me, too, baby girl," her father added.

"You guys are making me blush," Anna giggled nervously, and sure enough, her face was the color of a tomato.

"You're so modest," Ronnie teased. "You created all these amazing pieces. Own it!"

"Yeah, yeah," Anna said, and I could tell her nerves were getting to her. Her shoulders had gotten more and more tense as the minutes ticked towards 7:00.

"Why don't you all have a look around before it gets crowded in here. There's some champagne on a table near the back."

As the crowd dispersed, Anna leaned into my side. "Thank you," she said, her voice low. I kissed the top of her head and held her, knowing that was all she needed from me in that moment. "Thank you for everything. For being there for me when I didn't deserve it

243

and for never letting me go."

I looked down into the hazel eyes I fell in love with fourteen years ago. "You deserve everything."

"I want to show you something," she said, pulling away from me and taking my hand. She led me around a corner to a wall that held only one charcoal sketch.

"When did you do this?" I gasped.

She shrugged a shoulder. "I snuck a little in here and there when you were at work."

"It's amazing." I was looking at a black and white sketch of us—Anna and me—as kids, lying on the grass, looking up at the stars. The intricate details of the piece made it look like a black and white photo, not a drawing. It was titled "I Love You."

"This was when--"

"I first told you I loved you," I finished for her. She smiled and squeezed my hand. "I'm buying it."

Anna chuckled. "I didn't expect anything else."

I faced her, palming her cheeks and looking into her eyes. "I love you. I've loved you since I was fifteen years old, and I love you even more today. Thank you, Anna. Thank you for being my best friend, my lover, my wife, the stepmother to my daughter, and the mother of my son. Thank *you* for everything, and thank *you* for never letting *me* go."

I leaned in and kissed her then, repeating all those things I'd just said using my body instead of my words. Later tonight, when we got home, I'd do it again.

And again.

And again.

THE END.

Playlist

Here Without You – Three Doors Down
Closer to You – Adelitas Way
My Heart I Surrender – I Prevail
Last Stand – Adelitas Way
Out of My Head – Theory of a Deadman
Pass Slowly – Seether

Acknowledgements

I'm always afraid I'll leave someone out, so I'll start from the beginning...thank you Judi Perkins of Concierge Literary Designs and Photography for the beautiful cover that helped inspire the book and the title long before it was ever written. Thank you to my sister Tracy and brother-in-law Chris for answering my random Navy questions. Thank you to my betas—Nicole, Autumn, and Ginni—for praising this story when all I wanted to do was press delete, delete, delete. Thank you to my editor, Aimee, for doing such awesome work, for reading my mind, and for making me laugh—Pocket Jill, it's been a while! Thank you to Natasha for proofreading and for listening to every single b*tch and moan that comes out of my mouth. Seriously lady, you're a rock star. Oh, and thanks for tolerating me throughout the promo process! Read Review Repeat takes such good care of me! Thank you to Colleen and crew at Itsy Bitsy Book Bits for taking care of the review tour—your well-oiled machine had me resting easy. To all the readers and bloggers on my review team, you all rock! Thank you for taking on this assignment. Thank you to the bloggers who shared the reveal and the release. And finally, to all the readers who took a chance on this story, I hope you enjoyed Anna and Ryan.

xoxo Jennifer

About the Author

Jennifer was born and raised on Long Island, in New York. She relocated to North Carolina in 2002, where she met the love of her life. They got married and live their happily ever after just outside of Charleston with their fur-kids: a spoiled rat terrier, a cat who thinks he's a dog, and a cat who think she's an MMA fighter. When she's not reading or writing, she works a day job in an office, and is an evening graduate student, pursuing a degree in clinical counseling. She enjoys amateur photography, travelling, and music...it's a bonus when she can combine all three. She independently published her debut novel, *Our Moon (JACT 1)*, in June 2015.

Connect With Me

Email: jenniferlallenauthor@gmail.com
Website: www.jenniferlallenauthor.com
Facebook: www.facebook.com/jallenauthor
Twitter: https://twitter.com/AuthorJenniferA
Mailing List: http://eepurl.com/b4LjgD

Also by Jennifer L. Allen